Dr. John Polis

———— ///////// ————

# HOW TO PRODUCE ABUNDANCE IN YOUR LIFE

## The Kingdom Secrets Jesus Taught His Disciples

———— ///////// ————

JOHN POLIS MINISTRIES

"Putting the Word into the heart of man."

How to Produce Abundance In Your Life
by Dr. John Polis

Printed in the USA

Library of Congress Control Number: 2010925392
ISBN: 978-0-9826954-0-1

Prepared for Publication By

PALM TREE
PUBLICATIONS

Palm Tree Publications is a Division of Palm Tree Productions
www.palmtreeproductions.net
PO BOX 122 | KELLER, TX | 76244

To Contact the Author
JOHN POLIS MINISTRIES
PO BOX 1007 | Beaufort, SC 29901
843.322.0363 | drjohn@rfiusa.org
www.rfiusa.org

# ACKNOWLEDGEMENTS

I wish to express my gratitude to members of our ministry team who have co-labored with me in the preparation of the manuscript for this book.

My thanks goes to Ben Hoffmaster for cover design, Mrs. Susan Marotta for editing, Mrs. Theda Turner for typing, and Dorene Wright for the Chapter Study Guides. These wonderful Christian people devoted time and talent to this project, and may God bless each one of them *abundantly*. I also wish to say thanks to our friends at Palm Tree Publications who really are commited to helping authors get their message out. They go the extra mile as partners in the process. Another "God Bless You" to Todd and Wendy.

Dr. John Polis
March 2010

# CONTENTS

Appendix

---

ANYONE WHO
DESIRES CAN
BE ABUNDANTLY
PRODUCTIVE
IN LIFE.

—Dr. John Polis

---

# FOREWORD

Abundance is a sparingly used word in today's culture. Instead, what we see in the world today is excess. Excess is not abundance. Excess in and of itself has a negative connotation of being lavish, but heaping only upon ourselves. Excess is the perversion of abundance.

God's purpose has never changed with regards to abundance. He is El Shaddai which means *more than enough*. In other words, abundance. He wants us to be fully supplied and thoroughly furnished so we can be God's instrument of blessing in the earth. Abundance is God's means for us to be lavishly blessed with enough left over to lavish on others. It's a promise far too few of us have dared to believe.

With stunning simplicity, Dr Polis has sequentially illustrated the biblical "how-to" for abundance with re-markable and persuasive order. He has skillfully detailed an instruction that will help to light the path for anyone serious about producing the abundance promised in the Word of God. In light of the financial upset occurring in our world, *How To Produce Abundance In Your Life* is not only timely, it is vital.

This book is nothing short of line-by-line tutoring from a great man of God and I, wholeheartedly, recommend it as a must-read for anyone who dares to live by Heaven's economy.

Pastor David Crank
www.FaithChurchStLouis.com

# PLANTING THE SEED OF THE WORD IN YOUR HEART

In John 15:7 Jesus made a profound promise. Jesus keeps His Word. He said, *"If you live in Me and My Words live in you, you will ask what you desire and it shall be done for you."* What a tremendous revelation of the potential in your relationship with God... to have what you desire! Then, in verse eight, Jesus says, *"By this My Father is glorified that you bear much fruit, so shall you be My disciples."* He is saying the fruit, the result, of your living in Christ and God's Word living in you, is a very productive prayer life in which God gives you the desires for which you trust Him. In other words, out of the relationship of your abiding in Him and His word abiding in you, you become very fruitful and productive.

A person who produces abundantly for the kingdom of God is earmarked as a disciple of Jesus, not simply a Christian believer. There is a big difference between a believer and a disciple. Believers are people who accept Christianity as their faith. They believe in Jesus as opposed to Mohammed or somebody else. Disciples are people who have made Christ their life; they live the Christ life, a sanctified life not of this world. An abundantly fruitful life is the product of disciples, not believers. John 17:16-19 accounts Jesus talking to His Father about disciples. He describes disciples as those who the Father gave Him out of the world. He says they have accepted and obeyed God's Word and that "glory came to Him through them" (Could there be any greater compliment?). Jesus was praying this when He was about to leave the world. He knew the disciples would remain to carry on His work, so He asked His Father to protect them from the evil one by the power of His own name, and to give them the fullness of His joy.

So it is disciples—the people who live in Christ and in whom God's Word lives, who have the promises of John 15:7-8 and John 17:8 fulfilled in their lives. God grants them the desires of their hearts, protection, and a joyful, abundant life. Jesus' final prayer for the disciples was, "*Sanctify them by the truth; your Word is truth*" (John 17:17). He knew that living this productive life is a result of the seed of the Word being planted in our hearts. He knew that spiritual productivity is dependant on the divine principle of seedtime and harvest.

**SPIRITUAL PRODUCTIVITY IS DEPENDANT ON THE DIVINE PRINCIPLE OF SEEDTIME AND HARVEST.**

God's plan for productivity is the same in both the natural realm and the spiritual realm. How does God make this earth productive in the natural realm? Genesis 8:22 says, "*While the earth remains, seedtime and harvest, cold and heat, winter and summer, day and night, shall not cease.*" The Bible says that God makes the earth, the natural realm, fruitful through seedtime and harvest.

Look at Isaiah 55:8, "*For My thoughts are not your thoughts, nor are your ways My ways, says the Lord. For as the heavens are higher than the earth, so are My* ways higher than your ways and My thoughts than your thoughts. For as the rain comes down and the snow from heaven and do not return there but water the earth and make it bring forth and bud that it may give seed to the sower and bread to the eater, so shall My Word be that goes forth out of My mouth; it shall not return to Me void, but it shall accomplish what I please, and it shall prosper in the thing for which I sent it." This scripture clearly tells us that God makes the earth productive through the principle of seedtime and harvest. It then tells us that the spiritual realm works the same way, "...so shall my word be..."

All truth is parallel. For any truth you see in the natural realm you can find a parallel truth in the spiritual realm. The spiritual realm is the kingdom of God, the realm of the Holy Spirit. In Mark 4:26 God illustrates the principle of seedtime and harvest applied in the spiritual realm. "The kingdom of God is as if a man should scatter seed on the ground and should sleep by night and rise by day and the seed shall sprout and grow and he himself does not know how. For the earth yields crops by itself; first the blade, then the head, after that the full grain in the head; but when the grain ripens, immediately he puts in the sickle because the harvest has come." God causes us to be productive in the spiritual realm the same way He causes the earth to be productive in the natural realm; through seedtime and harvest. I can guarantee you there is no other way.

When Jesus said, "Seek ye first the kingdom of God and His righteousness and all these other things will be added unto you" (Matthew 6:33), He was saying, "If you understand the principles of seedtime and harvest, you will understand the kingdom of God. He also said, "If you understand the law that governs your productivity, seedtime and harvest, then all these things are going to be added unto you." How are all these things going to be added unto you? By operating the law of seedtime and harvest in your life just as God applies the same law in the earth to bring forth fruit and bud, and to produce a harvest. Jesus declared there is no need to worry about where you will get food, clothing and shelter. He said, "Just seek the kingdom." How do you seek the kingdom? Again, "so is the kingdom of God as if a man should cast forth seed into the ground, sleeps and rises night and day, *it springs and grows up he knows not how."* You seek the kingdom by learning to operate in seedtime and harvest in your life.

The principle which governs productivity of life on earth and in God's kingdom is seedtime and harvest. Once we learn that and operate in it, we will bring forth an abundant harvest; a fruitful, productive life. Anyone who desires can be abundantly productive in life. God is no respecter of persons. The principle doesn't work for one person and not for another person.

## ANYONE WHO DESIRES CAN BE ABUNDANTLY PRODUCTIVE IN LIFE.

If you plant seed in the ground, the ground doesn't care who put the seed in it. It doesn't make any difference who plants it, it's going to produce. The ground is no respecter of persons, the seed is no respecter of persons, and God is no respecter of persons. This will work for whosoever will, but you have to work within the process. It will not work automatically outside of the process. If you start operating the laws of seedtime and harvest every day, you can plan that a year from now your life will become more abundantly productive, producing a harvest such as you have never had.

## Every Harvest Begins With Seed

Let's look at the ingredients of the process. Every harvest begins with seed. The Bible says, in 1 Peter 1:23 that *"we are born again, not of a corruptible seed, but of an incorruptible seed, by the Word of God that lives and abides forever."* The Word is the seed; *"If you live in Me and My Word lives in you..."* (John 15:7). God plants His seed in us. When you are born again, you are born of the incorruptible seed. God's seed brings regeneration in your life. You grow according to genetic makeup and now you have been re-gened. That is regeneration. You are now born of the incorruptible seed; you have been re-gened by God. Now you will produce everything God has and is in your life because you have been regenerated by the incorruptible seed of the Word of God. So what will your harvest, the full-grown seed, look like? It is going to look like the image of the invisible God, like the Word that was made flesh. The seed which was full grown was Jesus. He was the harvest of the seed of the Word, and that is your future.

Jesus was abundantly productive. He turned His world upside down. He cast out devils, healed the sick, raised the dead, cleansed the lepers, and calmed storms. He produced an abundant harvest. He knew how to get money too. He even retrieved money out of a fish's mouth. You have to catch something to get money out of it. God pays fishermen. God pays you for catching fish, when you are a soul winner who wins people to Jesus. God will bless you phenomenally for leading people to Christ.

## Good Ground

From where does God produce an abundant harvest? He produces it from the ground. The dirt is the ground in the natural realm. The ground in the spiritual realm is your heart; your spirit man where the Word of God is sown. In Matthew 12:33 Jesus said, *"Either make the tree good and it's fruit good or else make the tree bad and it's fruit bad, for a tree is known by it's fruit."* He then pointed out the fruit of the Pharisees, "*Brood of vipers, how can you being evil speak good things? For out of the abundance of the heart the mouth speaks. For a good man, out of the good treasure of his heart, brings forth good things, and an evil man, out of the evil treasure of his heart, brings forth evil things.*" "Bringing forth" refers to the harvest of the Word seed that He has sown in our hearts. You cannot bring forth a harvest where you have not sown any seed. People wonder, "Why is God blessing those people? Why does it seem everything they touch prospers? Why do they walk in health, and why do favor and opportunity come to them?" It is because they are getting a Word seed harvest. The seed has matured because they are operating the principles of seedtime and harvest. "*A good man brings forth good treasure out of his heart.*"

The Bible tells us what the good ground, "*But the ones that fell on the good ground are those having heard the Word with a noble and good heart, keep it and bring forth fruit with patience*" (Luke 18:5). So now we find that the soil is our heart, our spirit man, and the seed is the Word. The soil in which God sows the seed is our heart. Next there is a soaking.

## Soaking is Required for Growth

This soaking is described in Psalm 1:1-3. *"Blessed is the man who walks not in the counsel of the ungodly nor stands in the path of sinners, nor sits in the seat of the scornful. But his delight is in the law of the Lord, and in His law does he meditate both day and night. He shall be like a tree planted by rivers of water."* Growing into a tree is the result of something. We are no longer just a seed; we have grown into a tree which *"brings forth fruit in season"* and *"whose leaf also shall not wither and whatsoever he does shall prosper."* Why? Because a tree planted by water is constantly immersed and soaking in water. The result of the continual soaking is tremendous growth. In the spiritual realm we grow when we immerse ourselves in the Holy Spirit. We immerse ourselves in the Holy Spirit

THE RESULT OF THE CONTINUAL SOAKING IS TREMENDOUS GROWTH.

when we come and worship and when we spend time alone with God soaking in His presence. When we continually immerse ourselves in worship and in His presence, we are living near the river of living water.

## Prepare your Ground

The ingredients for an abundant harvest are seed, good soil, and ample soaking. Now let's consider the first step in the course of action toward an abundant harvest. You begin by preparing to plant the seed of the Word in your life. Before you can plant seed you must take all of the weeds out of the garden plot. You do not plant seed in the midst of weeds. Psalm1:1 says, "*Blessed is the man who walks not in the counsel of the ungodly, nor stands in the path of sinners, nor sits in the seat of the scornful.*" This is weeding. Do not stand listening to the counsel of the ungodly. The original translation says, "*Don't take the advice of the ungodly, those who are morally wrong.*"

I see Christians taking the advice of morally corrupt people in the world. For example, the world will tell you it is okay to live together and not be married, and Christians believe it. They tell you it is okay to live together because God understands trial marriages. There is no such thing as a trial marriage. That is using and abusing people, getting the privilege without the responsibility.

But the world is morally corrupt, and the church seems to want to walk in the counsel of the ungodly by listening to the morally corrupt world. They cannot have blessing while walking in that ungodly counsel. You should not establish your values from the world's system, but instead, be transformed by the renewing of your mind. Christian values come from the Word of God and from godly people. So you cannot get your values from watching TV. You may get some values, but they will not be the right ones. Why would anybody want to sit and listen to somebody's failure week after week?" But many Christians do and then ask, "Can you help me with my problems?" When you come to me and say, "Can you help me fix my problems?" I will take you to Psalm 1 and say, "Are you willing to do that?" If you are not willing, I say, "I'm sorry, I can't help since you are not willing to weed your garden, to stop taking the counsel of this world, and its value system."

Morally corrupt people tell you, "It's okay to just have one beer, or, it is okay to take one pill or to smoke just one reefer." The world will tell you it is okay to have a little bit. Let me tell you, compromise demands increase. If you drink one you are done. You are going all the way in. You must shun the very appearance of evil; you must weed your garden. Do not listen to the counsel or advice of morally wrong people.

**COMPROMISE DEMANDS INCREASE.**

The second part of Psalm 1:1 says, *"Walk not in the counsel of the ungodly or stand in the way of sinners."* The way of sinners is a well-traveled road. In Bible days people walked along these roads in groups. One person would teach the others as they walked. The picture here is a group of sinners all walking together. God says, "Don't walk in the counsel of the ungodly or stand in the path of sinners." Get off the road; quit walking with that crowd on their way to sin. Separate yourself from them. Do not get on their path. You cannot travel with them. You can work with them and you can invite them to dinner to get them out of their environment and into yours. Don't avoid them, but go after them, on your ground. Don't go onto their ground.

Weeding our garden to gain an abundantly productive life means we stop following the advice of the morally corrupt, stop walking with the crowd on the road to sin, and, third, stop sitting in the *"seat of the scornful."* Sitting in the seat of the scornful means you set yourself in a position of a judge over other people's lives by mocking and scoffing them. The word judge means to use your mouth on people. The Bible teaches us to judge with righteous judgment, but it does not teach us to mock, scorn, and scoff people, condemning them in our judgment. So He says, *"Don't walk in the counsel of the ungodly, stand in the way of sinners, or sit in the seat of the scornful."*

## Plant the Seed of the Word in Your Heart

You have to weed your garden by plucking these things up, out of your life. This is step one of increasing your harvest and having an abundantly productive life. Next, we plant the seed of the Word in our heart. We have to come to this place of planting the seed. I have been a pastor a long time. I have seen that a lot of people are unbalanced because they just go after the Spirit. They pray, praise, and worship, but their river is a mile wide and only an inch deep. They have a flow of the Spirit in their life, a lot of water, but no Word—no revelation, no real deep planting of the Word of God. If you are going to be a balanced Christian, you must seek God, get full of the Spirit, and have Holy Ghost encounters, but you also have to bury the Word of God in your heart. To the same extent you stay in the rain of God, stay in the Word of God. To be productive you have to have both.

> IF YOU ARE GOING TO BE A BALANCED CHRISTIAN, YOU MUST SEEK GOD ... YOU HAVE TO BURY THE WORD OF GOD IN YOUR HEART.

Psalm 1:2 says, "*But his delight is in the law of the Lord and in His law does he meditate day and night.*" There is personal responsibility for having an abundant harvest, for living a productive life, and for seeing the fruit of God manifested in your life. You have to meditate in the Word of God day and night. In Hebrew, "to meditate" means "to be in the Word continually." The New Testament church took the Word of God seriously. Today many people can take or leave the Word of God. But Joshua 1:8a says, *"This Book of the law shall not depart out of your mouth, but thou shall meditate on it day and night."* The early church continued steadfastly in the apostles' doctrine teaching. Every time the apostles were teaching, the people of the early church were there. They *"continued steadfastly,"* not casually, not according to convenience, but they were steadfast; they adhered to the Word of God and to the teaching.

These people were serious about the Word of God and you and I must be serious about it too. You know you are serious about the Word when you obey what the Holy Spirit has written there. Joshua 1:8b reads, *"This Book of the law shall not depart out of your mouth but you shall meditate therein day and night, that you may observe to do according to all that is written therein;*

for then you will make your way prosperous and have good success." This is not just for a chosen few, for some especially favored people who have a charmed life. God does not operate that way. He is no respecter of persons.

God operates and produces abundance through the law of seedtime and harvest. In the natural realm we understand the illustration of how He causes the earth to bring forth and bud. In the spiritual realm it works the same way. He doesn't work any other way. Seedtime and harvest is your key to abundance in life. "Learn to live in the law of seedtime and harvest." God said "And I will bring forth fruit and I will show you My abundance in your life, every day of your life."

Stay in the Word continually, every day. If you read three chapters a day, you'll read through the Bible in a year. Carry your Bible with you. Have a couple of copies; your big Bible (your sword) and a small New Testament (your dagger). Keep your dagger in your pocket or in your purse. Keep your Bible with you. Get scripture memorization cards to keep in your pocket.

You will use your time and your energy on what matters to you. If the Word of God matters to you, you will find time to memorize it so you can meditate on it day and night. How can you meditate on it day and night if you don't memorize it? You can't read the Word while driving the car or feeding the baby. The Bible says you have to write the Word of God in your heart, *"I have hid thy Word in my heart that I might not sin against Thee"* (Psalm 119:11). You must get the Word of God in your heart by memorizing the scriptures. You have to meditate in the Word day and night, but you can't meditate on it unless you memorize it.

The word "meditate" means to speak out loud, to mutter it, to be in it continually. Go around muttering the Word of God all day long. When I get up in the morning I mutter, I speak, the Word of God to myself. I say, "Praise God, I'm a workmanship of God, created in Christ Jesus unto good works today. I am of God, and whosoever is of God has overcome the world, and this is the victory that overcomes the world, even our faith; I'm a world overcomer today. I put on the Lord Jesus Christ and make no provision for the flesh today to fulfill the lust thereof. In Him I live and move and have my being. The anointing of God abides in me and leads me and guides me in all truth and shows me things to come and teaches me all things, I have the mind of Christ, I know what Jesus knows." Meditate in the Word of God; speak it, think it, envision it, get it before your eyes day and night; that is the key.

## MEDITATE IN THE WORD OF GOD ... THAT IS THE KEY

## Three Stages to Productivity

Here is the biblical description of the process of preparing for your abundant harvest. Jesus said, "*The kingdom of God is as if a man should cast seed into the ground, he sleeps and rises night and day, it springs and it grows up, first the blade, then the corn, then the full corn in the ear.*" These are the three stages to productivity, first the blade, then the corn, then the full corn in the ear. Everything in the kingdom is in three phases; babyhood, childhood, and manhood; Jesus, Holy Spirit, Father.

Meditating on the Word of God gives you information. Gaining information is the blade, the first phase. Next,

Planting the Seed of the Word in Your Heart

—

25

**THESE ARE THE THREE STAGES TO PRODUCTIVITY—**

**FISRT THE BLADE, THEN THE CORN, THEN THE FULL EAR OF CORN.**

you take the information and meditate on it. As a result of the meditation, the second phase, the corn, comes. The corn is revelation. Revelation causes the information to come alive by the Spirit of God in your heart. You think about it and think about it until, all of a sudden, the Spirit of God shows you exactly what He means in that verse of scripture. We say, *"The entrance of Thy word giveth light"* (Psalms 119:130).

Finally, we want the full corn in the ear. The full corn is impartation. The Word of God is life to those who find it. Proverbs 4:20-23 says, "My son attend to My words, incline your ears to My sayings, let them not depart from before your eyes, keep them in the midst of your heart," because "they are life unto those who find them and health to all their flesh." Life is the impartation which comes from the revelation of the Word of God. For example, when you meditate on the subject of faith, you memorize and meditate on scriptures on faith. You get the information (the blade) which, all of a sudden, becomes revelation (the corn); the Holy Ghost shows you what faith really is and how it works. Then, all of a sudden, impartation (the full corn) of the Spirit of faith enters your spirit. It's no longer just a formula; it's the Spirit of faith at work within you.

2 Corinthians 4:13 says, "*We believe therefore we speak, we all having the same Spirit of faith.*" That impartation of life came from revelation of the Word of God. Many Christians never get this deep. They struggle to believe because they are not operating the principle of seedtime and harvest. They do not weed their garden, or meditate on and memorize the Word of God until information becomes a revelation—until revelation releases impartation, making God's Word part of them. Impartation means the Word is now part of me. This is how you learn to live and walk by faith. When the revelation comes, the full corn in the ear has come. When the impartation comes you are now living by the Spirit of life that is in you; you are living by the faith of God that is on the inside of you. You are no longer trying to believe, but instead, the life of God is manifested in you.

Jesus said in John 6:63, "*The flesh profits nothing; it's the Spirit that gives life. My words are Spirit and they are life.*" The harvest comes when the Spirit of the Word is imparted to your spirit man and faith becomes a part of you. It is not something you try to do, or something you try to practice but faith is a part of you. You don't have to remember to speak the Word, "*Out of the abundance of the heart the mouth speaks.*" The Bible says, "*A good man, out of the good treasure of his heart, brings forth good things.*"

When you meditate on the scriptures about the love of God and memorize 1 Corinthians 13: 4-8, you get it on the inside of you. "*Love is patient, love is kind, love is not arrogant, does not brag, does not act unbecomingly, does not seek it's own way, it's not provoked, doesn't take into account a wrong suffered, bears all things, believes all things, hopes all things, endures all things.*" Meditate on the love of God and information becomes revelation. The blade becomes the corn and then you get that revelation impartation in the spirit of life. Love becomes a part of you, an impartation. Love is now who you are—you don't have to try to be nice anymore; love is who you are.

Healing is the same way. When you meditate on and memorize scriptures on healing, you sow the seed of the Word of God in the garden you weeded. You are planting the seed of the Word of God in your own heart; the soil that God is going to use to bring a spiritual harvest into this world. Meditate on all the scriptures on healing; get the information and then revelation will come. Once revelation comes, impartation will come; then, life and health will be in you. *"The same Spirit that raised Christ from the dead quickens your mortal body"* (Romans 8:11). Health and life will be on the inside of you. You may have to weed something out of your life for that health to manifest. I once had to weed out coffee to be free from acid reflux.

I have a money harvest in my life as a result of sowing the seed of the Word of God concerning finances. I am now a money magnet. I meditated on the Word concerning finances for many years. The information became revelation and the revelation became impartation. Now financial favor is a part of me; an impartation. I haven't worried about money for a long time. Money just comes to me. No more begging, no more cheating, no more pleading. Even Christians trying to get ahead take the world's advice and cut corners a little bit, but you cannot get ahead that way. Just operate the seedtime and harvest principle of planting the seed of the Word of God in your life; let it become a full harvest and impartation. There is an impartation of whatever that Word is carrying. The Word is Spirit and life. You have to get to the stage, through

**THE WORD IS SPIRIT AND LIFE.**

meditation, where information becomes revelation, which becomes impartation so that the Holy Spirit imparts the life of the Word and the Word becomes a part of you. From then on it's all natural; it's just who you are and you reap the blessings of benefits and advantages of every kind.

For example, once we signed a contract on a condominium on a Friday. The realtor said, "It may be Monday before you get a response." So I grabbed the realtor's hand to loose the anointing and we prayed.

The Spirit of God immediately moved in our favor. Thirty minutes later the realtor called and said, "You have a verbal agreement already!" He was astounded it had happened so quickly and at my price. The impartation of His Word brings the favor of God into our life.

## The Word Brings Forth The Harvest

Jeremiah 15:16 says, "*The words were found and I did eat them, and thy words became unto me the joy and rejoicing of my heart.*" When the Word of God gets inside of you, you may not feel the rain of heaven that day, but your spirit holds a harvest of joy. Do you know how joy manifests itself? Strength. You may not be laughing but you'll be strong in the face of adversity. Strength, the joy of the Lord, will arise inside of you. Strength is a harvest of the seed of the Word in your life.

Proverbs 4:20 says, "*My son attend to my words, incline your ear to my sayings, don't let them depart from your eyes, keep them in the midst of your heart.*" Why? "*...for they are life*" (Proverbs 4:22). Impartation comes when I have meditated. I heard it, I kept it before my eyes, I meditated upon it, it got in the midst of my heart, and revelation came. Then, as the revelation came, impartation came. Life was imparted to me. It is health to all my flesh.

Now notice Proverbs 4:23; *"Keep your heart with all diligence."* That means your heart is a garden so the weeds could grow back, *"and choke out the Word."* Keep your heart with all diligence because, *"For out of it spring the issues of life."* The Amplified Bible says, *"Out of the heart come the controlling forces of life."* You rule from your heart. The controlling forces of life are faith, love, and wisdom. They are a harvest from a seed sown in your life; an abundant harvest of the power of the Holy Ghost. The Power of the Holy Ghost proceeds from you when you speak a word. Gifts of the Holy Ghost, signs, wonders, and miracles generate from you when you speak His words. Didn't He say you would be like a tree planted by rivers of water, bringing forth fruit in your season? Your leaf does not wither. Wither means to bring disgrace. When you plant the Word of God in your heart, you will never bring disgrace to yourself, to others, or to God. When you live in the harvest of the life God has imparted into you, you walk as Jesus walked. You grow up in all aspects into Him who is the head, even Christ. The same controlling forces which were at work in Jesus are at work in you; the same love, the same faith, the same wisdom, the same power.

Remember the woman with the issue of blood who touched the hem of His garment? The Bible says that *"Jesus perceived virtue had flowed out of Him."* He didn't pray for her. She just came up and got in the atmosphere of Jesus' life, in His anointing in faith, and received a miracle from the issues of life which flowed out of Him. The same life forces which sprang out of His Spirit can spring out of you.

Jesus was the Word that was made flesh and grew to become the full-grown tree. You were born again of the same incorruptible seed so you were predestined to be conformed to the image of Christ. God is maturing you into another Jesus, another full-grown tree. Jesus said, *"My Words are Spirit and they are life."* When He said, *"The flesh profits nothing, it's the Spirit that gives life, My Words are Spirit and life,"* He meant, "I walk in revelation; My Words are Spirit, not just information. I walk in revelation, and also beyond: I walk at the level of impartation."

Take this Word, *"Keep your heart with all diligence for out of it flow the forces of life"* (Proverbs 4:23). Weeds will try to grow back. Somebody will offend you and there will be a weed unless you get it out right away. Weeds will attempt to grow back to choke the Word of God out of your heart; then your crops of faith, love, wisdom, favor, the harvest of the seed, and the impartation will be choked out, unless you *"keep your heart with all diligence."*

# STUDY GUIDE

## Chapter One Summary

*Jesus desires for his disciples (people who have put aside everything and made Christ their life), to have a fruitful, productive life. God's plan for productivity is the same in both the natural and the spiritual realm.* **This principle is seedtime and harvest. The ingredients for this process are seeds, good soil, and water.** *In the natural, you weed the garden, till the soil, plant the seeds, and water the garden. Your garden then begins to produce.*

*For example, if you plant seeds for corn, your garden produces the blade, the corn, and finally, the full ear of corn. In the spiritual realm, you* **prepare your ground by weeding out the unglodly things in your life;** *you separate yourself from the world. Next you* **plant the seed** *(which is the Word of God) into your ground (which is your heart). Then you* **water that spiritual garden** *by immersing yourself in the*

*Holy Spirit through worship and spending time alone with God. You **read the Word** and gain informatin (which is the blade). Then you **meditate upon that Word** and revelation (which is the corn) comes alive in your heart. The **revelation of the Word brings forth impartation** (the full ear of corn) which makes the Word a part of you. You are no longer trying to believe—you do believe! **The Word is alive within you.** The Word, which was made flesh, is Jesus.*

———— ⁄⁄⁄⁄⁄⁄⁄ ————

*Fill in the blanks. There is an answer key provided on page 139 at the end of this book.*

1.  Believers are people who have accepted Christianity as their faith, but disciples are people who have made _____ their life. By living a sanctified life, they become _____ and _____ . This spiritual productivity is due to the divine principle of_____ and

_____ .

2. Psalms 1:1-3 tells us, "Blessed is the man who walks not in the _____ of the ungodly, nor stands in the path of _____ , nor sits in the _____ (this is weeding). But his delight is in the Law of the Lord, and in his law he _____ both day and night (planting the seed). He shall be like a _____ planted by _____ of water, that brings forth his fruit in his season; his leaf also shall not wither; and whatsoever he doeth shall _____ (we mean grow by immersing ourselves in prayer and worship).

3. We learn in 1 Peter 2:3 that, "We are born again, not of a corruptible seed, but of an _____ seed, by the _____ of God that lives and abides forever." The Word is the _____ and the seed brings regeneration in your life. Your harvest will look like the image of _____ who is the Word made flesh.

4. The three stages to productivity are the blade
   (which is the _____ ), the corn
   (which is _____ ), and the full ear
   of corn (which is the _____ ). The
   Word is now part of you. Go and bring forth your
   harvest.

   _____ NOTES

# PLANTING THE SEED OF FAITH WITH WORDS

Genesis 8:22 reads, "*While the earth remains seed-time and harvest, cold and heat, winter and summer, and day and night shall not cease.*" This is good news. "As long as the earth remains there will be seedtime and harvest."

We have already seen that planting the seed of the Word in our heart is the way God produces abundance in our life. God works in the spiritual realm the same way He does in the natural realm. This passage of scripture gives us the secret to how God makes the earth productive—seedtime and harvest. There is no productivity on this planet in the natural realm except through seedtime and harvest. Every year we look forward to this cycle because seedtime and harvest is how we know we are going to eat next year.

God brings productivity to our spiritual life using the same parallel to natural productivity. Seedtime and harvest is the system God uses to bring abundant productivity into our spiritual life. This system brings a harvest of revelation, healing, gifts of the Spirit, favor, wisdom, and everything you and I need to have an abundant life.

Many people wait for God to impart abundant life apart from this process of seedtime and harvest. They wait, but it never happens. They think they can just get in a prayer line so God can touch them and cause some-thing supernatural to happen apart from their operat-ing in the principle. But people receive the abundant harvest and productivity of life through the principles of the kingdom. We could experience an extended spir-itual revival in which we continually shouted, danced, jumped, hollered, and rolled on the floor. But after that is all over, we have to learn to live by the Word of God. As we know from church history, there are seasons. The

Bible says, "*Ask ye in the time of the latter rain for rain*" (Zechariah 10:1). We ask for rain and it rains—but if it keeps raining, and raining, and raining—we will have a flood.  Nothing gets a chance to grow in a flood. So it's not all about rain, rain, rain, rain every day because we would all drown.  No, it will rain until we get enough water and then we will grow.  During the times God sends rain we rejoice while having encounters and ex- periences.  Then there are times when God just wants us to get the seed of the Word into our heart so that rain can produce something in our life.  If there is no seed in the ground all that rain will not produce any- thing but a goosebump.  All that rain without seed in the ground produces only valleys and ravines. There will be no harvest or fruit.  We have to have the balance of Spirit and truth in our lives. It is just as important for you to get the Word in your life as it is for you to get rain. Don't be a flaky, carnal Christian who picks and chooses. Keep a balance.

WE MUST HAVE THE BALANCE OF SPIRIT AND TRUTH IN OUR LIVES.

Get in the rain and get soaked, but also get in the Word and grow.

## Principle and Phenomenon

There are two main precepts in the kingdom, **principle** and **phenomenon**. The phenomenon is a spontaneous sovereign act of God. You are just there when it happens and it makes you happy. We do not live by phenomenon but by principle. We cannot live from one phenomenon to the next. We learn to live by the principle. Jesus said, *"Man should not live by bread alone ..."* (Matthew 4:4). What, an occasional phenomenon? Most Christians are waiting for an occasional phenomenon and in between these experiences, nothing is growing. They get rain, but since there is no seed in their life, they produce nothing. It takes some effort to get the seed in your heart so that when you get rain you produce a harvest. Mark 4:26 shows us how God makes us productive. *"So is the kingdom of God, as if a man should scatter seed on the ground; and should sleep by night and rise by day and the seed should sprout and grow up. He himself* does not know how for the earth yields grain by itself, first the blade, then the head, after that the full grain in the ear. But when the grain ripens, he immediately puts in the sickle because the harvest is come." God makes us productive—abundantly productive through seedtime and harvest. The sooner we learn that this is the fundamental law of the kingdom of God and the sooner we begin to operate in seedtime and harvest, the sooner we see our lives producing an amazing abundance.

Matthew 12:35 says, "A good man out of the good treasure of the heart bringeth forth good things." So, you are productive because something good comes out of your heart, that is, out of your spirit man. It comes because you deposited something good in there. Faith, love, and wisdom grow out of your heart. Supernatural power grows out of your spirit man.

You must plant a seed to understand the principle of the kingdom and produce abundance in your life. What happens when the seed is planted? "Night and day, while he's asleep or awake, the seed sproouts and grows, but he does not understand how it happens" (vs. 27). The

Bible says, "*He sleeps by night and day, the seeds springs and grows up, he does not know how.*" He does not have any concern about it because he cannot comprehend it. Do you have God figured out? You just trust Him to do what He said, even though you don't know how.

## Put Something in the Ground

So the first principle of kingdom abundance is this, **you have to put something in the ground**. You begin to activate the principle in your life by planting seed. Then, since you don't know exactly how it's going to come about, you rest. For example, you may plant the seed for healing in your life, thinking your healing is going to happen one way, but it happens another way. Perhaps you expect the healing in five minutes, but instead you get better gradually over a period of time. Your job is to plant the seed, but because you will never understand totally how it will produce fruit in your life, you rest. When you really enter into rest with your seed of faith in

**YOUR JOB IS TO PUT SEED IN THE GROUND—NOT TO WORRY ABOUT HOW IT WILL PRODUCE.**

the ground, you do not worry or wonder how it's going to happen. The farmer knows the seed is going to come up in its time and that the earth is going to yield fruit of itself. God has set it up that way. Get the seed in the ground and the earth produces by itself.

The farmer's main responsibility is to **get the seed in the ground**. Can you imagine how silly it would be for a farmer to spend a million dollars to irrigate 1000 acres and never plant any seed? How many Christians do that? How many Christians spend all their time praying, fasting, and getting soaked with the Holy Ghost, and yet they don't know ten scriptures? Their ground is totally irrigated, but there is nothing there to grow because they did not put the seed of the Word of God in their lives.

If there is anything that has helped me have any measure of productivity, it is giving the Word of God first place in my life all the time. If I don't get a goose bump that's okay, I'm going to get some Word. When you go to church you need to have the attitude that it is okay if you don't get a goose bump that day because you are going to get some Word.

I have been a pastor for a long time. I have seen hundreds and hundreds of people coming and going. I've seen that only a few people ever really become productive and live the abundant life. The problem is not with God's system. The Bible tells us in the parable of the sower that there are four types of ground and only one out of four is good ground—only one. The good ground is the one who hears the Word of God, keeps it, and patiently brings forth fruit. That is one out of four Christians. I've seen that out of a hundred people, twenty-five of them are going to produce fruit. Twenty-five of them will take the Word of God seriously and give it first place in their lives. The rest just get goose bumps and wait for a phenomenon to occur. They take the things of God casually and lightly. Only one out of four Christians really understand that God works by principle and law, laws and principles.

## GOD WORKS BY PRINCIPLES AND LAWS.

I am here today because of the law of seedtime and harvest. I have had a harvest of healing in my life. The devil has tried to kill me



How to Produce Abundance in Your Life

several times, but he just can't do it because I have my harvest of healing. The Word I have sown has gone from information to revelation to impartation. Divine life just keeps springing out of my spirit; going through my body and correcting afflictions.

That is the only way to live, but most people do not understand this. They will not read the Bible, pray, meditate on, or memorize scripture. They don't take it seriously. They don't buy Kenneth Hagin mini books to carry in their back pocket. They say, "No, I don't have time for that. I don't like to read." I say, "Well, I guess you just like to die early." Hosea 4:6 says, "*My people are destroyed for a lack of knowledge.*" I cannot help you if you will not help yourself.

A young man once came up to me at the altar and said, "My marriage is all messed up; what can you do for my marriage?"

I said, "Nothing."

He looked at me and his expression was clearly saying, "Huh? Pastors are not supposed to say that!"

I looked him in the eye and said, "I can do nothing for your marriage, what can you do for it?"

"Me?" He said, "Do you mean *me*? *I'm* supposed to do something?"

I said, "I'll tell you what I'll do. I'll come to your house and tell you what *you* are supposed to do." So I went to his house and told him what he could do to save his marriage. He did nothing. He did not want to change.

How badly do you want your life to change? You will show everybody how badly you want it to change by what you do. I'm tired of seeing people dying, broke, depressed, and demonized when we have a system that (for those who are willing to work it) will produce a hundred-fold return harvest of health, healing, prosperity, peace, joy, and love.

Many people have grown up without discipline, training, or mentoring. These people become irresponsible and take on a welfare mentality that says, "Let the government do it for me. Let the church do it for me. Let somebody else do it for me." Every one of us is responsible to bring forth an abundant harvest of fruit in our lives. God wants everybody to win. He is no respecter of persons—He is a respecter of faith. It takes effort to obtain faith in your life, but you can have it.

**IT TAKES EFFORT TO OBTAIN FAITH IN YOUR LIFE, BUT YOU CAN HAVE IT.**

When Jesus said, "*I will build My church*," He was not talking about building an organization. I am not interested in building a great church organization; I'm interested in building some great people. The church will be great when the people are great. A great church is not a large number of people who still need somebody else to do their praying and their delivering for them. I want to see a church of people who have great faith, great love, great revelation, great power, and great authority.

Jesus *made* His disciples. He put everything He had into them. Pastors are supposed to be mentors who feed the flock of God to make disciples of them. Jesus wanted His disciples to be 100-fold producers; to have abundant, productive harvests. In John 15:16, Jesus said to His disciples, "*You have not chosen Me but I have chosen you, and I have ordained you.*" Look what it says, "*I have ordained you that you should bear much fruit, and that your fruit should remain, that whatsoever you ask the Father in My name He may give it to you.*" Bearing fruit was His vision for His disciples. Bearing fruit is His vision for you and it is my vision for you. I want everyone healed, I want them free from welfare and into a good job. I want everyone to have a business of some kind and thousands of dollars to sow and invest in the Gospel. I want everybody driving a new car and living in a nice house. I want everybody to have it all, but we're not going to get it all unless we understand the kingdom and the principles of the kingdom and learn to live by them. **We cannot be lazy Christians and still get a harvest.** You will never see a lazy farmer who has a big, wealthy farm. Farmers work very hard. You have to work at being a Christian. You cannot be a lazy Christian.

Luke chapter 17:5-6 reads, "*The apostles said to the Lord, 'Increase our faith.' He replied, 'If you have faith as a mustard seed, you would say to this mulberry tree, be pulled up by the roots and be planted in the sea and it should obey you.'*" The disciples asked for more faith and Jesus told them to use the faith they had. Next, He told them to look at faith as a seed they should plant. *"So is the kingdom of God, as if a man should cast seed into the ground; and should sleep, and rise night and day, and the seed should spring and grow up, he knoweth not how. For the earth bringeth forth fruit of herself; first the blade, then the ear, after that the full corn in the ear"* (Mark 4:26-28).

## How Do We Plant the Seed of Faith?

Faith, as a seed, must be planted. How do we plant the seed of faith? What did Jesus say? **You plant faith seed in the spirit realm by speaking your faith.** You plant the seed of faith with words. Next, you must leave the seed in the ground. That means you never change what you spoke. How many people would expect to get a harvest off of a seed they sowed if they dug up the seed every week? Once you plant that seed of faith by

**YOU PLANT THE SEED OF FAITH WITH WORDS.**

speaking the word of faith, you have to wait on that seed to grow and produce.

This is how the kingdom operates. First, you look at faith as the seed. Then, you plant it by speaking. Next, you guard what you say. Do you talk gloom and doom, despair and agony? Are you repeating what the news is saying, what the devil is saying, what your body is saying, or what your brain is saying? Your brain will tell you the opposite of what is happening. No, you get that seed in the ground by speaking the Word of God. Then keep your seed in the ground by not changing what you have said.

This principle is illustrated in Jesus' life. *"Now the next day when they had come out from Bethany He was hungry. Seeing from afar off a fig tree having leaves, He went to see if perhaps He would find something on it, but when He came to it He found nothing but leaves, it was not the season for figs"* (Mark 11:12). Obviously, this tree had a chemical imbalance or something because the leaves were evidence that the fruit should also be there. This tree was producing leaves out of season; it wasn't in God's order. So the Lord said, *"Let no man eat fruit from you ever again"* (Mark 11:14). There was something wrong with that tree so He cursed it by speaking a word of faith, *"Let no man eat fruit from you ever again."* The story continues, *"Now in the morning as they passed by they saw the fig tree dried up from the roots. Peter, remembering, said to Him. 'Rabbi, look, the fig tree which you cursed has withered away.' And Jesus answering said to them, '***Have faith in God***, for assuredly I say to you, **whoever says to this mountain be removed and be cast into the sea and does not doubt in his heart but believes that those things which he says will be done, he will have whatever he says'* "** (Mark 11:20-23 *emphasis added*).

You see, Jesus operated by the kingdom. That fig tree dried up from the roots because of the principle of the kingdom of God. Your cancer can dry up because of the principle of the kingdom of God. Your heart disease can leave because of the principle of the kingdom of God. Your poverty can turn to abundance because of the principle of the kingdom of God. Your wayward children can become sanctified and set on fire for God. All this comes to pass by the principle of the kingdom of God—not by wringing your hands and worrying.

This will change your life. In the next verse, Jesus said, "Therefore I say unto you, what things soever you ask when you pray believe you receive them and you will have them." The reason Jesus said that is because these verses go together. When you pray, you believe, you receive what you pray for, and then you speak what you believe you have received. Speak what you *want*, not what you *have*. Jesus spoke what He wanted. He wanted the fig tree dried up from the roots. That is what He spoke and that is what He received.

Mark 11: 23 mentions believing only once, but mentions saying three times. Read it again, "For assuredly I say to you, whosoever says to the mountain be removed and cast in the sea and does not doubt in his heart, but believes those things that he says, he shall have whatsoever he says." What does that mean to you? It means you need to multiply your speaking the Word of God into your life. **Get the seed of the Word of God in the ground and don't change your confession.** "Hold fast the confession of your faith without wavering, faithful is He that promised, He also will do it" (Hebrews 10:23).

One of my favorite scriptures to confess when the devil attacks my mind is, "*And may the God of peace Himself sanctify you completely and may your whole spirit, soul and body be preserved blameless at the coming of our Lord Jesus Christ*" (I Thessalonians 5:23). Then I confess, "*He who calls you is faithful who also will do it*" (v. 24). I walk around saying those verses over myself. I say, "Lord, I thank you that you preserved my whole spirit, soul (that is my mind, will, and emotions) and body blameless. At your coming I will be whole. Faithful is He that said

> FAITHFUL IS HE THAT SAID IT— HE IS ALSO GOING TO DO IT

it—He is also going to do it. When you want a harvest of peace in your mind, when you want to be free from confusion, plant the seed of the Word of God by faith. Do this by speaking this scripture over your life.

## Faith is Built by Understanding Authority

Another illustration of speaking faith is the account of David and Goliath. David operated in this principle of the kingdom. He defeated his giant with the principle of seedtime and harvest. He put a seed of faith in the ground and beat Goliath.

> *So the Philistine said to David, "Am I a dog that you should come to me with sticks?" And the Philistine cursed David by his gods. And the Philistine said to David, "Come to me and I will give your flesh to the birds of the air and the beasts of the field." David said to the Philistine, "You come to me with the sword and the spear, and javelin, but I come to you in the name of the Lord of Hosts."*
>
> *I Samuel 17:43-44*

David was saying, "I am a representative of Almighty God. I'm the only one standing up here willing to represent God; as a covenant partner with God." All the other warriors were in the trenches. They had a covenant with God too, but there was only one person who would stand up and say, "Okay, Goliath represents the armies of the enemy (the bad guy). I'm going to represent the good guy, Almighty God. So I come to you in the name of the Lord!" David was God's representative in covenant with Him on behalf of all Israel. He understood that he was in covenant and was the representative of the covenant of God, so he said, "But I come to you in the name of the Lord of hosts, of the armies of Israel whom you have defied, this day." This is his seed going in the ground. Then David said, "This day the Lord will deliver you into my hand" (1 Samuel 17:46).

How could he be so sure? Because God had already promised in the covenant to be everything David needed Him to be. David could speak by faith because he already understood the covenant. We need to understand that we have a covenant with God, and that

**WE CAN SPEAK BY FAITH WHEN WE KNOW OUR WORDS ARE BACKED UP BY GOD'S COVENANT.**

we can speak by faith because we know our words are backed up by that covenant. That is why we can say, "By His stripes I was healed." That is why we can say, "Everything I lay my hand to prospers." That is why we can say, "With long life He satisfies me and shows me His salvation." We can say, "I'll go to my grave in full vigor like a shuck of corn in its season." And, "Great is the peace of my children for they are taught of the Lord and nothing *shall offend them."* This is why we can plant seeds of faith and speak the Word of God; because **we have a covenant behind us** and we are representatives of that covenant. Just like David, we come forward with our faith.

When David said, *"I come to you in the name of the Lord, and this day the Lord will deliver you into my hand and I will strike you and take your head from you"* (I Samuel 17:46), he was very detailed. He put God on the spot. A fifteen-year-old boy against a nine foot giant was not expecting to do this in his own power. No, he was out there bragging on God. He knew **his** Giant was bigger than **their** giant. *"Greater is He who is in us than he who is in the world"* (I John 4:4).

You can stand in the face of cancer and tell the cancer, "I'm a representative of Almighty God; I have the covenant behind me. Based on that covenant, in the Name of Jesus, I command cancer to leave my body."

David came without a sword in his hand, but he had a sword of another kind. He knew the covenant he had with God and that God had committed to him all His power and ability. He knew God could defeat not just Goliath, but the whole Philistine army! So he declared, "And this day I'll give the carcasses of the camp of the Philistines to the birds of the air, and the wild beasts of the field are going to have lunch today, that all the earth may know that there is a God in Israel" (v. 46).

"So David prevailed over the Philistine with a sling and a stone, and struck the Philistine and killed him, but there was no sword in the hand of David" (v. 50). The Holy Spirit wrote that fact, "There was no sword in the hand of David," to emphasize to us that David's sword wasn't in his hand—he had a sword in his mouth. According to Ephesians 6:17, you have a sword in your mouth too. It is called the sword of the Spirit, the Word of God. When you speak a word of faith, that sword cuts. The sword goes to the root of a thing and cuts it loose.

If we could all learn to live by the principle of seedtime and harvest, we would be producing an abundant harvest of miracles, healing, prosperity, peace, joy, and deliverance in our families. God has already put the system in place to bring abundant prosperity into our lives. It is called seedtime and harvest.

## You Must Plant the Seed— You Must Speak in Faith

**You have to plant the seed of faith.** David went out and planted his seed of faith. Jesus said, *"Whosoever shall say ..."* David understood the principle so he got up and *spoke*. When I pray over people, I *speak* over their lives. I *speak* what I want to see take place in their lives—as children of God, and as Christians. I *speak* revelation knowledge, financial abundance, and impartation.

In Mark 5:25 we read about the woman with the issue of blood who came to Jesus. *"When she heard of Jesus she came in the press behind and she said, 'When I touch Him I'll be healed.'"* When she said those words, she put the seed in the ground. When she reached the hem of His garment, it was harvest time.

**Speak the Word.** *"If you have faith as a grain of mustard seed you would **say** to the sycamore tree, be* thou plucked up and cast into the sea, and it should obey you" (Luke 17:6). Jesus went on to say, "And nothing shall be impossible to you." Why? Because the seed will reproduce after its own kind; the seed will produce a harvest. **The principle of the kingdom of God will work in your life.**

In 1983 God spoke to me and said, "Change the name of your church." The name was *Calvary Open Bible*. He said "Change it to *Light of Life World Outreach Center*." Do you know what He was telling me to do? He was telling me to plant a seed of faith, to speak it—to call the things that were not as though they were. So I said it, and we were laughed at. People thought it was a big joke that we had that big sign, with that big name but only 75 people. Since then, this ministry has touched thousands of people internationally. We obeyed. We spoke the word and that seed went into the ground. We started acting on the Word of God, operating the principle of the kingdom, and entered into rest. Within six months after I changed the name of the church, I was invited (supernaturally) to Kenya.

I went and had a revival with the Full Gospel Churches of Kenya. I preached for their youth camps for the next seven years. Thousands of young people (as many as 2,200 to 2,500 in each meeting) were baptized in the Holy Ghost. I preached to the Full Gospel Churches all over the nation of Kenya. I was the only man to speak twice in their 50th anniversary celebration. On that occasion in Nairobi, there were 30,000 people in that stadium. I had a harvest that day ... and that was just Kenya.

Next we went to Liberia, Malawi, Tanzania, Romania, Bulgaria, and Scotland. We preached every year for ten years in Scotland, bringing restoration truth to the top leading charismatic church in that nation. Thousands of peoples' lives changed. I met a young man who was preaching in South Africa. He said, "I'm a Kenyan, I was in your youth camp in Kenya when you preached a message back in the late '80s. God called me that day. Now, as a result of the message you preached at that youth camp, I pastor a church in Zaire."

We have had some fruit as a result of our seed, but I'm getting ready to take another launch in the spirit.

I am preparing—first a blade, then the corn. I haven't had the full corn in the ear yet. I'm getting ready for a harvest in this world like I've never seen before. I believe God is going to do it. He said, *"You plant the seed. You sleep and rest, and you don't know how it's going to bring forth fruit of itself."*

The beauty of the principle of the kingdom is that **anybody can reap 100 fold**. Anyone who learns to live not by a phenomenon but by the principle of the Word of God can produce an abundant harvest.

# PLANTING THE SEED OF FAITH WITH WORDS

# STUDY GUIDE

## CHAPTER TWO SUMMARY

*Planting the seed of the Word in our heart is how God produces abundance in our life.* There is no productivity in the natural or spiritual realm without seedtime and harvest. We cannot bring forth a harvest of healing, gifts of the spirit, wisdom, etc. without this principle operating in our life.

*We must plant the seed of the Word in the ground.* We cannot do this without reading the Bible, meditating upon that Word, and memorizing Scripture. Dancing, jumping, and hollering may feel good, but it doesn't produce anything if the Word of God has not been planted in our hearts.

*Standing on the Word is what produces results in our life.* "The kingdom of God is as if a man should scatter seed on the ground, and should sleep by night and rise by day, and the seed should sprout and grow, he himself does not know how. For the earth yields crops by itself; first the blade, then the head, after that the full grain in the head, but when the grain ripens, immediately he puts in the sickle, because the harvest has come." *(Mark 4:26)*.

**This is the fundamental law of the kingdom of God: seedtime and harvest.** *A lazy farmer will not produce a prosperous farm. Lazy Christians will not produce a powerful church with great authority.*

**We must plant the seed of faith, speak the Word over the situation, and hold fast to (not change) our confession.** *Continue always to speak the Word.*

**We have a covenant with God—our words are backed up by that covenant. This enables us to speak by faith.** *If we will understand that we live by the principle of the Word of God and not by a spiritual phenomenon, we can produce an abundant harvest. We can speak to our mountain, "Be thou removed and be cast into the sea," and it will be done!*

*Fill in the blanks. There is an answer key provided on page 139 at the end of this book.*

1.  Genesis 8:22 tells us that as long as the earth remains there will be _____ and _____. This is the principle of the kingdom of God.

2.  There are two main precepts in the kingdom: _____ and _____. _____ is a spontaneous, sovereign act of God. We do not live by this precept but by _____.

3.  We activate the seed of faith with our _____.

4.  If we need healing in our life, we plant the seed of the _____ into our heart and by _____ we speak the Word into existence. Hebrews 10:23 tells us to "Hold fast the _____ of our _____

without _____ , for He is faithful that

promised."

5. We can plant seeds of faith and speak the Word of God

because we have a _____ with God.

Our words are backed up by that _____ .

———————————————————————— NOTES

# PLANTING THE SEED OF MONEY FOR FINANCIAL HARVEST

We have studied planting the seed of faith with words and planting the seed of the Word in our hearts. These are fundamental principles of the kingdom of God and are the means by which God produces abundance in our lives. Every one of us wants to be abundantly productive. These principles are how you accomplish this. Abundance does not come automatically, but comes as a result of operating in the principles of the Word of God.

In this chapter, we will explore planting the seed of money for a financial harvest. The scriptural base for

69

this chapter is Psalm 35:27. It reads, *"Let them shout for joy and be glad who favor My righteous cause and let them say **continually**, 'let the Lord be magnified'"* (*emphasis added*). Notice that they are to speak continually—not infrequently—but as part of their daily confession that the Lord be magnified (that is, that God be made bigger). They are instructed to make God bigger instead of making problems bigger. Magnify the Lord by saying everyday, *"He has pleasure in the prosperity of His servant,"* and *"My tongue shall speak of your righteousness and of your praise."* How often are we to do this? Continually—all day long. If we want to be abundantly productive and see the principle of seedtime and harvest work in our lives, we have to do this and do it from our hearts.

## Plan for Your Harvest

You must plan for your harvest. In planning for your harvest you must **determine to serve God.** Psalm 35 declares that God takes pleasure in the prosperity of the people who are serving Him—the people who have made a decision and are determined to be the servants of God. What is a servant? A servant is someone who obeys the master. An obedient servant gives the master what he wants. A servant waits to hear the next command. How do you know when you have become a servant of the Lord? You are a servant when you posture yourself before God, waiting to hear the next command: the next instruction for your life.

Paul said that he became a servant immediately when he met Jesus and was slain in the spirit (Acts 9). The first words out of his mouth were, *"Lord, what would you have me to do?"* Upon speaking those words, he became the servant of the Lord and his life began to be abundantly productive from then on. We never hear of Paul or Peter having to rededicate their lives. We never hear of any of these disciples having to go back to the altar. No, when they decided to accept Jesus, they determined from that moment they were going to be the servants of God. Determine today that you are going to serve God because He delights in the prosperity of His servants.

## DETERMINE TODAY THAT YOU ARE GOING TO SERVE GOD.

# Expect Your Harvest

The first aspect of planning for a harvest is to **expect it.** I expect abundance in my life. I am a money magnet. I expect money because I'm operating in these principles. If I am doing what the Bible says, I have a right to expect. If I am not doing this, if I am *not* a servant of God, I don't have any right to expect. So, **when I *am* serving God, I have every right to be confident and expectant.**

# Determine Servanthood & Stewardship

The second aspect of planning for a harvest is determining. We must *determine* to be God's servant. We must also *determine* to be good stewards of all we have. **This determination to be God's servant and to be a good steward is fundamental to prosperity.**

*"Let a man so consider us as servants of Christ and as those entrusted with the secret things of God. Now it is required that those who have been given a trust must prove faithful"* (1 Corinthians 4:1-2). Paul is declaring that we are the servants of Christ and stewards of the

mysteries of God. As stewards, it is required that we be found faithful.  There is no place in those verses for any other option. **Faithfulness is a requirement of stewardship.**

**FAITHFULNESS IS A REQUIREMENT OF STEWARDSHIP.**

If you are going to expect a harvest you have to *determine* to be a good steward of all you have. Actually, everything we have belongs to the Lord—all that we have and all that we are (even our bodies) belongs to God.  The Bible says, *"We are the temple of the Holy Ghost whom we have of God which is in us and we're not our own, but we are bought with a price"* ( 1 Corinthians 6:19). You are bought with a price, you belong to God.

How do you take care of your body?  Whenever I start abusing mine the Holy Ghost in me says, "Hey, how about taking care of My house?  My shutters are falling off and My pipes are leaking.  Take care of My house because I plan to live here a while, I don't want to have to move out." **Be a good steward of your temple.**

# Use What You Have

Practice being a good steward of everything you have. This includes information you have received from the Word of God. **Use what you have learned to multiply and increase.** The key to multiplication in your life is to use what you have, *"To him that has shall more be given"* (Matthew 3:1). *"He that waters shall be watered himself again in return"* (Proverbs 11:24). The key to getting more is to use what you have—give away some of what you have, and you get more!  Because I have found this to be true I never turn down an opportunity to minister. When somebody calls me, I go because I know I'm going to give something that I have and that God will give it back, *"good measure, pressed down, shaken together and running over"* (Luke 6:30).  I keep giving away the revelation I have and keep getting more revelation.

**Be a good steward of all you have.** This is one of the keys of abundant productivity, *"it is required that you be found faithful."* For example, consider your car. Do you take care of your car?  Do you change the oil and wash your car regularly? Is your car still wearing last summer's dirt? Is the interior filled with fast food wrappers and empty water bottles. If so, that is not being a good steward. You may think this has nothing to do with living a life of abundance, but it does. I want you to have much. I want you to have a new car. I want you to have the best car. Faithfulness is a requirement of stewardship—stewardship of your car, your home, your finances, your family, your revelation ...

God said, "He delights in the prosperity of His servant." What are you doing with what you have? These fundamental things are easy to miss. People pray for God to give them abundance, and God says, "Have you seen your car lately?" You say, "Lord, I believe I receive a hundred-fold return," but then never check the air in your tires. It is your responsibility to make sure all the tires have the same amount of air pressure in them so they don't wear out at 10,000 miles instead of lasting the 60,000 miles they were designed for. The extra $400 you will now have to spend for tires was $400 you could have given to bless someone in need, or to finance a kingdom project. This is the stewardship God requires. These "little foxes" spoil the vine (Song of Solomon 2:15). Realize that

**God is paying attention to these little things.** What about your home? Do you have closets you have to stand back to open because everything falls out on you when you open the door? What is your attitude about your wardrobe? Is it, "I don't really care. I go to Goodwill. I'm not that much into it," or do you want a really nice wardrobe? When you realize you are a king and a priest, you will stop shopping at Goodwill. I thank God for Goodwill. It is there meeting a need for people, but if you have a "Goodwill mentality" you don't have a "Bible mentality." The Bible says, "*You are a king and a priest unto God*" (Revelation 1:6). You have to get a royal mentality and begin expecting to wear nice clothing.

How does this start? First, take care of the clothes you have. Take your clothes off and hang them up. This sounds like Home Economics 101, but I am illustrating the reason people do not prosper. **They do not prosper because they do not become good stewards as God required.** We have to acquire the mentality that

PEOPLE DO NOT PROSPER BECAUSE THEY DO NOT BECOME GOOD STEWARDS AS GOD REQUIRES.

everything we have belongs to God. When we realize that He ultimately owns everything, we start to take care of everything as a steward. Have you ever loaned your car to somebody and then watched them peel out as they drove off? You probably said, "Oh God, send a dozen angels with my car. Why did I do that?" When we ask the Lord for something and He sees us abuse the possessions He has lent us, He gets the same idea.

I have several nice vehicles. A car dealer once said to me, "Dr. John, I like to get your used cars because you take care of them." My cars are clean inside and out and I change the oil regularly. I didn't always have nice cars. I bought used ones and cleaned them up and took care of them, and then God put me in beautiful, brand-new, top-of-the-line cars. This principle is critical. **You have to determine to be a good steward of all you have before you can be abundantly productive.**

## Do Not Be Idle

These are keys to abundant productivity. We are considering how to plan for a harvest. **The next key is to determine to not be idle.** Paul admonished the

Christians in Thessalonica not to be idle. He said, "But we command you brethren, in the name of our Lord Jesus Christ that you withdraw from every brother who walks disorderly and not according to the tradition which he received from us, for you yourselves know how you ought to follow us" (2 Thessalonians 3:6-12). This means we should follow the spiritual leadership, "for we were not disorderly among you nor did we eat anyone's bread free of charge." You cannot look for a free ride. Paul didn't, instead he "... worked with labor and toiled night and day that we might not be a burden to any of you, not because we do not have authority." Those leaders could have said, "Hey, we're here as God's servants, you're supposed to take care of us." Instead their attitude was to be an example, they were going to work night and day plus minister. "But to make ourselves an example of how you should follow us, for even when we were with you, we commanded you thus, if anyone will not work, neither should he eat; for we hear that there are some who walk among you in a disorderly manner, not working at all" (vs. 9). Paul was shocked to learn that there were Thessalonian Christians who didn't work, but were "busy bodies." (A busy body has time to get into other people's business because they are not working and do not have enough to do.) Paul calls this an abomination.

"Now those who are such we command and exhort you through our Lord Jesus Christ that they work in quietness and eat their own bread" (vs. 12). **Anyone who wants to be abundantly productive should not look for a free ride in the kingdom of God.** We cannot be parasites living off others. The Bible says we are supposed to eat the bread that we earn by working and have enough left over to feed someone else.

Many people today have excuses for not working—they are idle. Some people have a physical disability so they just don't work. You can work with your body and you can work with your mind. If your arms and legs are disabled, you can still use your brain. You can start a business with just your brain. There is always a way.

Other people in our society have a welfare mentality. They want benefits without responsibility. Somebody has to be responsible—somebody has to pay the bills.

I want to be one of the people who provides, one who pays the bills. **Every Christian ought to be productive.** If you have a physical disability, I am not going to sympathize with you unless your brain is also disabled. If you cannot think, then we will take care of you. If you can think then you can work with your mind—there is no excuse not to work somehow unless you are totally disabled. There is always a way.

## Start Somewhere!

Paul said, *"But concerning brotherly love you have no need that I should write to you, for you yourselves are taught by God to love one another. And indeed you do so toward all the brethren who are in Macedonia. But we urge you, brothers, that you increase more and more in love, that you also aspire to lead a quite life, mind your own business, work with your own hands as we commanded you"* (1 Thessalonians 4:9-11). Now notice how God rewards hard work. *"That you may walk properly toward those*

GOD REWARDS HARD WORK.

who are outside and that you may lack nothing" (vs. 12). Those "outside" are the unsaved world. When you walk properly (work with integrity), they'll have a good opinion of you. God says, "*I'm going to bless the work of your hand.*" If you want to serve God you must have: 1.) a good reputation in the world, 2.) a good name as a Christian in the community, and 3.) work with your own hands. God will bless your business so you will lack nothing. He will give you a promotion and a raise. "*Despise not the day of small beginnings*" (Zechariah 4:10). Begin somewhere, even if it seems small or feels insignificant. As an example, let me tell you a true story about our Bible School Director, Ben.

I met Ben in Kenya when he was 18. He came out of a mud hut, wearing flip flops and rag-bag clothing. His uncle, who attended our Bible school there, had asked me to help his nephew by giving him something to do. So I hired Ben to trim the hedges around the school for a few schillings every month. He saved the money he made cutting hedges. When he had enough money saved, he asked me if he could start a little store on campus. He bought pencils, paper tablets, and doughnuts downtown and started selling those items to the Bible school students. He saved that money too. When I saw his industriousness I made him the keeper of the inside of the big house. We actually gave him a room in the big house because of his hard work—he determined to be a good steward.

I watched him clean the house and again save his money. Eventually he saved enough money to buy a little plot of land on which he built his mother a mud hut so she no longer had to live with a relative. At the mud hut, he planted some maize and saved the money he made from his crop. He still had his little store at the school and he still cleaned and cut hedges for me. Soon, I gave him a raise.

Later we hired some women to cook food for our 60 students and put Ben in charge of those cooks. Now he was the kitchen superintendent as well as everything else. I gave him another raise. He saved some money from that so he could go to a technical school in town. There he earned a diploma in business administration. I gave him some administrative responsibility in the office and another raise. Ben saved some more money and earned a computer diploma. The next thing I knew, he was wearing a three-piece suit. He had enterprises going on everywhere! I watched him blossom from a small beginning. Soon we made him the full-time Assistant Director of the Bible school.

Ben continued to develop and grow and is now the Director of our Bible school. We have 160 students enrolled in Bible school under Ben's direction. Ten years ago he was wearing flip flops and living in a mud hut. Now he wears a three-piece suit and owns a vehicle—which he bought with his own money. He is responsible for the operation of the whole budget of the school and for the 160 pastors enrolled there.

**Ben attended to the little stuff, and had a great harvest.** You have to attend to the little things.

## Four Things For Harvest

Determine to do these four things: serve God, be a good steward of everything you have, shun idleness, and find a way to work. Then you can plan for a harvest.

In Genesis 8:22, we see that God uses the principle of seedtime and harvest to produce abundance in both the natural and the spiritual realms. In the natural realm, the earth, we have a crop whenever we plant seeds. In the spiritual realm, God makes us abundantly productive the same way. In Mark 4 it says, *"So is the kingdom of God as if a man should cast forth seed into the ground, he sleeps and rises night and day, it springs and grows up, he knows not how, first the blade, then the corn, then the full corn in the ear, after that when the harvest is come he puts in the sickle."*

In the kingdom, God makes us productive spiritually so that everything we lay our hand to prospers through the principle of seedtime and harvest. First, prepare the ground by removing weeds. Next, plant the Word in your heart, and then activate the seed of faith with your words.

## Prepare Your Ground By Tithing

When preparing for a financial harvest, plant the seed of money. **Before planting the money seed, prepare your ground by tithing.** You have to plan for a harvest by making sure you are doing all the things I have mentioned.  So, **prepare for a financial harvest by bringing your tithe into the storehouse**. Let me show you what that means.  Malachi 3:8-9 says,

*"Will a man rob God?*
*Yet you have robbed Me.'*

*But you ask, 'How have we robbed you?'*

*'In tithes and offerings. You are cursed*
*with a curse for you have robbed*
*me, even this whole nation.'"*

What was the curse? The curse was famine and drought. God stopped up the heavens because they were withholding the honor from God.  It wasn't just the idea of money, but the tithe God had designated for a specific purpose.  It is His right and prerogative to do that. He has designated ten percent of our income for an eternal purpose.  Look at Malachi 1:6, "A son honors his father and a servant his master.  If I then am your Father where is My honor?  If I am a master where is My reverence?" The main problem in the book of Malachi was that people were dishonoring the Lord.  They dishonored Him by bringing Him sacrificial animals which were maimed and lame. They were also withholding their tithes and offerings, so God said, "A son honors his father, if I'm your Father where

**WHEN I BRING MY TITHE INTO THE STOREHOUSE, I AM HONORING MY FATHER.**

is My honor?" God wants to be honored. That is really all He wants from us. He wants us to honor Him because He is God. He does not want honor by legalism and law, but from a son's heart to a father. When I bring my tithe into the storehouse, I am honoring my Father because He has designated that ten percent for a divine purpose.

The amount of the tithe is a tenth, ten percent. **You cannot negotiate the tithe.** Three percent is not a tithe. Five percent is not a tithe. Seven percent is not a tithe. You cannot negotiate the amount because God set the amount. He said, "A tenth belongs to Me, because I need it, I have a purpose for it." The tithe is designated for the service of the sanctuary. According to the book of Numbers, it was designated so the priests would not have to work secularly. All the other tribes had secular work to do, but the priests' vocation was performing the service of the sanctuary, the place of worship.

The tithe was designated to provide resources for the tribe of Levi and the priesthood. The Aaronic tribe and Levitical priests did not have to work so they were free to provide worship for the whole nation. That was God's purpose. God designated ten percent as the amount—but a tithe is not a tithe unless it goes in the right place.

A lot of people say, "Well I give ten percent, but I give some of it here, some there … " Just because the total amount you give adds up to ten percent, that doesn't qualify it as the tithe. Tithe *is* an amount (10%) but it *also* has a designated place. The tithe is a designated amount and a designated place. Where is the place? The storehouse (Malachi 3:10). *"On the first day of the week, as God has prospered every one of you, lay in store"* (1 Corinthians 16:1-2). The New Testament people knew to lay in store proportionately from that which God had prospered them. It was a proportion, a percentage of their income. They knew to bring it to the corporate gathering and to lay it in store there.

The tithe is not only a designated amount by God, but it is also a designated place (which is the local church) where you assemble every week. The purpose of that tithe is to make sure that there is meat in the house; that the ministry of the local assemble can carry on in the community. If no one tithed you would not have a church to attend. **The tithe is three things: an amount, a place, and a purpose.** The right amount given in the right place and used for the right purpose constitutes a real tithe. This is tithe in the New Testament and you cannot negotiate it with God.

In Leviticus 27:30-32, the Bible says that they paid the tithe under the law, and that the tenth belonged to the Lord. Tithing was observed before the law was given by Moses. Abraham paid tithes (Genesis 14:20) to Melchizedek, who was a type of Christ. Jacob paid tithes (Genesis 28:22) when he was running from his brother Esau. He vowed to God, "Lord if you protect me from my crazy brother I'll give you ten percent of everything I gain." He knew giving a tithe to God put him under God's protective covering.

The tithe is the first obligation because God does not consider any seed sown until that tithe is in. First bring the tithe to the storehouse and, once the tithe is in the ground, something happens. "'Bring all the tithes into the storehouse, that there may be food in My house, and try Me now in this,' says the LORD of hosts, 'If I will not open for you the windows of heaven And pour out for you such blessing That there will not be room enough to receive it'" (Malachi 3:10).

## Prepare for Productivity

Malachi 3 shows us three ways the tithe prepares us to be productive. **The tithe opens the floodgates of heaven to *irrigate*, it rebukes the devourer to *protect*, and it *fertilizes* for abundance.** The first result of tithing is that you get rain. The Israelites were under a curse of drought for not honoring God. Nothing could grow. There is no use planting anything if there is no rain. In this way, the tithe is preparation. When you begin to tithe, you lift the curse. Now God can send rain onto your ground.

**WHEN YOU TITHE YOU LIFT THE CURSE.**

A farmer has to prepare his ground for harvest. We prepare our ground for financial harvest by bringing our tithes into the storehouse. Then God says, "Okay now farmers, you're preparing your ground, you're getting ready for seedtime and an abundant harvest, so I will irrigate your ground. We prepare—God makes it rain.

Second, God said, " 'And I will rebuke the devourer for your sake so that he will not destroy the fruit of your ground, nor shall the vine fail to bear fruit for you in the field,' says the Lord of Hosts" (Malachi 3:11). The tithe you bring to the storehouse lifts the curse, then God sends rain to water your garden. Next He protects your garden. "I will rebuke the devourer for your sake." A farmer sets a scarecrow in his garden, or puts a fence around it to protect it from birds and other animals. **When we bring our tithe into the storehouse, God puts divine protection on our ground—He protects our harvest and all our property.**

Jacob understood that the tithe would bring him protection from Esau. When you bring your tithe into the storehouse, you are placing yourself under God's protection. You are saying, "I put myself under the authority of God and under His delegated authority in the local church. I am bringing my tithe and placing myself under God's covering." Once you are protected you will not get robbed anymore. Don't you hate to go out to your garden where you have worked so hard and find that deer and rabbits got there before you? When you obey God by bringing your tithe into the storehouse, you will not have to fear anything that will plunder or rob your garden. **God is going to protect your ground.**

Third, God will fertilize your ground. *"All nations shall call you blessed and you shall be a delightful land, says the Lord of hosts."* That is productivity.

Tithing is not giving—offering is giving. Tithing is not a seed, it is stewardship—tithe belongs to the Lord. You cannot give something that does not belong to you. When you tithe you do not sow a seed, you just return the tenth part that the Lord requires, but you haven't given anything yet. The reason people can tithe and never really see any significant financial increase in their life is because the tithe is not a seed. An offering is a seed, and **increase comes from seed.**

If a farmer irrigates, puts up protection, and then fertilizes the ground but does not plant any seed, he did it all for nothing. Tithe is purely preparation for seedtime and harvest. Offerings are the seeds we sow. *"Give and it shall be given unto you"* (Luke 6:38). Giving is your offering. The tithe is not giving. The tithe belongs to the Lord, we just bring it back to Him. Whenever we receive money, whether as salary or through somebody giving us a gift, ten percent of that belongs to God. Give it to Him speedily because He waits for it. Only after I have returned that tenth to God am I ready to give.

**TITHE IS PREPARATION FOR HARVEST. OFFERINGS ARE THE SEEDS WE SOW.**

## Seeds of Money—Offerings

Luke 6:38 says, *"Give and it will be **given** to you."* How will it come back to you? The answer is in the rest of the verse, *"... good measure pressed down, shaken together and running over, it will be put into your bosom. For with* the same measure that you use, it will be measured back to you."

Understand that if you put ten dollar seed in the ground, you will receive ten dollars pressed down, shaken together, running over. But if you put a hundred dollars in the ground, God will measure it back to you in hundreds. When you use hundreds, He uses hundreds. If you use thousands, He uses thousands. Something happens when you hit that thousand-dollar level in your seed sowing. God returns thousands. That is what Jesus meant when He said, "For with the measure that you use, it will be measured back to you, good measure, pressed down, shaken together, running over."

This does not work for people who do not tithe. They might give $1000 to a TV ministry or a charity, but if they are not tithing to a local church, nothing happens. They might even say, "Well I gave and I got ripped off. Money is all those preachers on TV talk about." I like what John Avanzini said years ago, "I'm not trying to get money from you, I'm trying to get money to you." **We have to become givers.**

The majority of people have not really become givers yet. To some measure we all have, but not to the point of practicing the kind of giving that brings supernatural grace and wealth into our lives according to the Word of God. It's a challenge and it takes faith.

George Barna reports that the average church attendee gives 3.2 percent of their income—not a tithe. So, most people in the church do not tithe at all. In our ministry almost everyone who is a member tithes. We require tithing for membership. We have a great per capita income in our church because we teach people from the Word. Our people are prospering. They are getting more money because we are teaching the Word. They are giving more because they are getting more.

Paul says, in 2 Corinthians 9:6, "But this I say, he who sows sparingly will also reap sparingly, and whoever sows bountifully will also reap bountifully." That is the key. The mentality of people is to see how much they can get for how little they put in. But that is not right. "He who sows sparingly will reap sparingly, and he who sows bountifully will also reap bountifully." That is abundance. You have to get to the sowing stage and sowing comes after tithing. When we just tithe, we are not yet sowing. God uses the principle of seedtime and harvest to produce abundance in our life, so **we have to get past the tithe stage and to the sowing stage.** We have to get some seed in the ground, and the more seed you put in the ground, the more harvest you have coming.

## GIVE ON PURPOSE

2 Corinthians 9:7 says, "So that each one of us gives as he purposes in his heart." The tithe is designated by God, so we know Paul is not talking about the tithe. This giving is what we purpose in our heart (determine, decide) to give. When we want to challenge our own faith, we go beyond where we have gone before. We might purpose in our heart, "This month I'm going to sow $500 above my tithe." You must purpose in your heart to put financial seed in the ground beyond your tithe. I can honestly say that hardly a week goes by that I don't receive money from somewhere beyond my salary. I know that when I give, I am going to reap from planting that seed.

Paul continues, "*For God loves a cheerful giver, so let each one give as he purposes in his heart, not grudgingly as of necessity.*" Give cheerfully, not out of guilt, but out of a purpose in your heart. I want a harvest so I purpose to put some seed in the ground. "*For God loves a cheerful giver.*"

"*And God is able to make all grace abound towards you that you, always having all sufficiency in all things, may have abundance for every good work*" (2 Corinthians 9:8). What a verse! God has promised us **abundance** for every good work through His grace (which is God's enabling power). Giving releases grace. What produces "*good measure, pressed down, shaken together, running over*"? What hits that seed that makes it multiply? It's the grace of God.

**GIVING RELEASES GRACE.**

"*As it is written, 'He has dispersed abroad, He has given to the poor; His righteousness endures forever.' Now may He who supplies seed to the sower and bread for food, supply and multiple the seed you have sown and increase the fruits of your righteousness while you are enriched in everything, for all liberality, which causes*" *thanksgiving through us to God"* (2 Corinthians 9:9-11). He is saying, "You have plenty of money to give away, which causes thanksgiving through us to God."

All the people who have received the blessing of our giving are thanking God for it. Our Bible school in Kenya is thankful to God that we can send them money every month because our people give. Our people in Liberia, Malawi, and Bulgaria thank God every month because we have money to help them fulfill their purpose through their ministries. People are thanking God because the TV program is on. I often meet people who listen to our radio program. They tell me they really enjoy our program, and are fed by it. Someone sowed seed for that purpose. **Giving releases grace and favor.** God said, "I will make all grace abound to you, I will give seed to the sower."

## WHERE DOES SEED COME FROM?

Where does the seed come from? The seed is in the fruit. How does God give seed to the sower? The Bible says, first through labor (2 Thessalonians 3:10) so you can make some money (through gainful employment). From this money you tithe and you sow some seed. Then God gives more seed to you, the sower, through the fruit your harvest. Every time you reap a harvest, you've got more seed. If every time you reap a harvest, you take some of that seed and plant it, your barns will soon be filled with plenty to the point of overflowing. This is so basic and simple, but so powerful and true.

God uses seedtime and harvest to bring productivity in the natural and spiritual realms. There is not a realm that does not touch seedtime and harvest. To operate in seedtime and harvest you must do these four things:

- make sure you are a **good steward**,

- find some way to **work** no matter what your situation,

- bring your **tithe** into the storehouse,

- and **sow seed**—always increasing your measure because by your standard of measure it will be measured back to you.

# PLANTING THE SEED OF MONEY

## FOR FINANCIAL HARVEST

# STUDY GUIDE

## CHAPTER THREE SUMMARY

Abundance comes as a result of operating in the principles of the Word of God—the principle of seedtime and harvest. There is not a realm that does not revolve around this principle. **To be blessed financially, we must serve God, be a good steward of everything that we have, shun idleness, and find a way to work.**

Before we can plant a seed, we must prepare our ground by **tithing**. Tithing is ten percent of our increase and it belongs to God. We are to give our tithe to the local church we attend.

Once our ground is prepared, the next step for financial harvest is to **plant the seed of money**. A harvest comes from seed. **Our offering is our seed.** As we increase the amount of seed we sow, our harvest is increased. **Giving releases grace and favor.** God will give more seed to the faithful sower.

We are the church. The church is to grow and carry forth the Gospel throughout the world. Accomplishing this mission requires resources—money. **It is God's will for His people to be blessed financially.** God's people are to be an example to the world. We are blessed!

Fill in the blanks. There is an answer key provided on page 139 at the end of this book.

1. You have to plan and expect your harvest. First, you must become a _____ of God. He delights in the prosperity of his _____ . Second, you must be a good _____ . The determination to be a servant and a good steward is fundamental to _____ . God pays attention to how we take care of what we have because everything we have belongs to God. Next, we must work and not be _____ . II Thessalonians 3: 10 tells us that if we don't _____ we should not _____ .

2.  We can now plan for a harvest. We prepare our
    ground by _____ . The amount of the
    tithe is _____ . The place the tithe
    is designated for is the _____ . The
    purpose of the tithe is to make sure there is
    _____ in the storehouse—money to
    support the church.

3.  The _____ is a seed. II Corinthians 9:6
    tells us if we sow sparingly we will _____
    sparingly, and if we _____ bountifully,
    we will reap bountifully.

4.  Malachi 3: 1 0-12 tells us that if we pay our tithes that
    God will open the _____ of heaven
    and pour us out a _____ , He will
    rebuke the _____ for our sakes, and
    all nations shall call us _____ .

# HOW TO PLANT YOUR LIFE AS A SEED

We have surveyed seedtime and harvest and observed that all of life revolves around this principle. In the first chapter, we discussed how to plant the Word of God in your heart. The second chapter demonstrated how to plant the seed of faith with your words. Next, we learned how to plant financial seed for a money harvest. When Jesus taught that we reap what we sow, He was not speaking about money alone. Financial seeds are only part of the message. In this chapter we will examine how to plant your life as a seed.

John 12:23-26 reads, *"But Jesus answered them saying, 'The hour has come that the Son of man should be glorified. Most assuredly I say to you, unless a kernel*

103

of wheat falls into the ground and dies it remains alone, but if it dies it produces much grain. He who loves his life will lose it, and he who hates his life in this world will keep it for eternal life. If anyone serves Me let him follow Me, and where I am there My servant will be also. If anyone serves me, he My Father will honor.'"

## Absolutes

Jesus understood that there are absolute laws that govern life and He operated in those laws. We live in an age of relativism in which few people believe in absolutes. Without absolute laws, everyone becomes his own god—making and remaking thier own rules according to their own circumstances and individuality. This is the result of our culture throwing out the Bible which teaches absolutes. There are unchanging laws in the universe to which we must align ourselves. We must submit ourselves to these unchanging laws to get along in life.

**THERE ARE UNCHANGING LAWS IN THE UNIVERSE TO WHICH WE MUST ALIGN OURSELVES.**

# You Must Repent

Luke 13:3 states one of the laws which govern the universe, **"Except you repent you shall all likewise perish."** When He said *"except,"* it was an absolute. Unless a person repents he will not enter the kingdom of God, but will perish. The word *"perish"* is the word for lost. *"God is not willing that any should perish but that all should come to the saving knowledge of Jesus Christ"* (2 Peter 3:9). God does not want one person to be *"lost."* Jesus Christ came to seek and save that which was lost. The word *"lost"* is the same word for *"perish"* and means to lose something. When we lose something valuable to us, we are in grief until we find it. When something is lost it is no longer in your possession.

Before we are saved we are lost. That means we are not in God's possession. The Bible tells us that Satan is the god of this world and that lost sinners (those who are not in God's possession) belong to Satan. When Jesus died on the cross and shed His blood, that blood paid a price to redeem those who put their faith in His blood.

The word "*redeemed*" means "*to be bought back*" like when you go to the pawn shop and buy back something lost to you so it becomes your possession again. When Jesus died on the cross, He shed His blood. When you placed your faith in that blood He bought you back from Satan. At that moment you were no longer lost but became God's property once again. If you know what it means to be saved, you know what it means to celebrate and rejoice because you know how desperate you felt when you were lost. You know what it means to be out of God's possession—living in darkness, groping around for a light, trying to find your way, asking, "Why am I here? How did I get on this planet? What is my purpose?" All those questions get answered when you receive Jesus, repent of your sin, and accept Jesus as your Savior. When you receive salvation you allow the blood of Jesus to work for you, to redeem you so you become God's property once again.

1 Corinthians 6:19-20 says, "*What? Do you not know that your body is the temple of the Holy Spirit who is in you, whom you have from God, and you are not your own? For you were bought at a price; therefore glorify*

God in your body and in your spirit, which are God's."
**Do you know how precious you are to God?** He paid the supreme price, His Son's sinless blood to redeem you, buy you back and put you back in His possession. Once you became His property again, He sent the third person of the Godhead, the Holy Spirit, to live in you to take care of His property. He said, "*Holy Ghost, I want you in there taking care of that for which I paid a precious price. If it's in trouble, rescue it. If it's sick, heal it. If it's needy, provide for it. Take care of what belongs to Me.*"

You need to understand how valuable and precious you are and what it cost God to redeem you and get you back in His possession. Realize that He sent the Holy Spirit to take care of you, provide for you, lead you, guide you, and teach you. He lives in you. Isn't that glorious? Isn't that wonderful?

At the time of this writing, I have been a Christian for 36 years. For all that time I have known that God loves me so much that He bought me with a price—a price that cannot ever be duplicated again. Christ died once and for all, the just for the unjust, that He might bring us to God. His death does not need to be repeated because it was sufficient for all eternity. We have been justified by His blood. He has declared us, "not guilty." But the deal is this: *"Except you repent you will perish."* Unless you repent you will continue to be lost all your life, and if you die that way, you will be lost throughout eternity.

The only reason people ever go to hell is because they rejected His love, His mercy, and His grace. God does not want people to be in hell. God created hell for Satan and his angels. Some new-age gurus are preaching that there is no heaven and no hell. They are lost in the sauce. God help them and save them because they will split hell wide open if they do not acknowledge Jesus Christ as the way, the truth, and the life. *"No man cometh unto God but by Him"* (John 14:6). *"You shall all likewise perish."* Nobody escapes it—we must all repent.

## You Must be Born Again

Another absolute Jesus taught is, **"Except a man be born again he cannot see the kingdom of God"** (John 3:7). Why must we be born again? Because it's not what we do that causes us to be lost, it's what we are. We are all born sinners who by nature commit the acts of sin. That is why you cannot just go to a psychologist, follow a self-help program or practice behavior modification to become a better person. You will go to hell anyway because the crux of the matter is this: it's not what you **do**, but what you **are**.

Ephesians 2:1-2 reads, *"We were all dead in trespasses and sins, but He quickened us and made us alive together with Christ."* God recreates our spirit man as we pass from death to life. *"If any man be in Christ he is a new creation, old things pass away, behold all things become new."* I am not a pot smoker, a beer drinker, a porno indulger, a thief, or a liar anymore. I am the workmanship of God, created in Christ Jesus unto good works which God has beforehand ordained from the foundation of the world. I am a new creature in Christ. I am not an old sinner saved by grace. I **was** an old sinner, but now I **am** saved by grace—now I am the workmanship of God created in Christ Jesus unto good works. I am a new creature in Christ.

He said, *"You must be born again."* You must become a new creature in Christ, a partaker of His divine nature, or you cannot see the kingdom of God. In other words,

**YOU MUST BE BORN AGAIN TO SEE AND UNDERSTAND THE KINGDOM OF GOD.**

outside of knowing Christ, you stay spiritually blind to the kingdom of God. You must be born again to see the kingdom, to understand the realities of the kingdom of God, the Holy Spirit, and the supernatural power of God. You must be born again.

## A Vision for Harvest

In John 12:24 Jesus tells us, "*Except a kernel of wheat falls into the ground and die it remains only a single seed.*" These are absolutes that govern our lives. Jesus counted on the law of seedtime and harvest to make His life abundantly productive. If Jesus counted on that law to produce abundance in His life, you and I have to count on that law to produce abundance in our lives. John 12:24 also says, "*But if it dies, it produces many seeds.*" So, Jesus knew He had to die in order to get the harvest. He put His faith in a seedtime and harvest. You and I have to do the same thing. Look at Hebrews 12:1&2, to see what enabled Jesus to endure. He had a vision of the harvest. When you have a seed, you have a vision of a harvest because you know every seed reproduces after its own kind. Jesus knew if He sowed His life as a seed, the seed of His life would produce more seed of His life. But the sown seed has to die before there can be a multiplication of that kind of seed. New seed is a duplication of the seed which died. We reap what we have sown. If we plant an apple we don't get a pear.

**NEW SEED IS A DUPLICATION OF THE SEED WHICH DIED.**

**Jesus planted His life because He had a vision of a harvest.** What was the vision of the harvest? Hebrews 12:2 says, *"For the joy that was set before Him, He endured the cross."* Hebrews 12:1 tells us, *"Therefore we also, since we are surrounded by so great a cloud of witnesses, let us lay aside every weight and the sin which does so easily ensnare us; looking unto Jesus the author and finisher of our faith, who for the joy..."*

What does a farmer think about when he looks out at that field after he has planted it? He does not picture all those seeds dying in the ground, he pictures amber waves of grain. He looks out at that field, and thinks about his corn and wonders how many bushels he will harvest. He is seeing the harvest because the farmer believes in seedtime and harvest.

*"For the joy that was set before Him, (Jesus) endured the cross, despising the shame thereof, and He has sat down at the right hand of the Majesty on high."* Jesus had the joy before Him. What was the joy He was looking for? *"With many other words, He testified and exhorted them, 'Be saved from this perverse generation.' Then those who gladly received His word were baptized and that day about three thousand souls were added to them"* (Acts 2:40).

Here is the harvest. Jesus had joy picturing the day of Pentecost when the Holy Spirit would fall and herald in the salvations of thousands of people. What happened when they got saved? Did they just become church members? No, when they got saved, they became seed, capable of reproducing after their own kind. *"For who He did foreknow He also predestined to be conformed to the image of His Son that he might be the firstborn among many brethren"* (Romans 8:29). That man—Christ who was in the image of God, who died on the cross, and rose again from the dead—was a seed. In Him was the duplication, the multiplication of what He was. When we are saved, we don't become just Baptists, Methodists, or Pentecostals. When we are born again, we are a child of God—made in the image of God. We are born again, the workmanship of God, created in Christ Jesus unto good works. *"And as Christ is, even so are we in this world"* (I John 4:17).

## Duplicated in His Image

In the law of seedtime and harvest, what you sow you reap. The seed that went in the ground on resurrection day caused multiple resurrections on the day of Pentecost. Three thousand resurrections occurred. Those who were dead in trespasses and sins were quickened, made alive together with Him.

The same power that raised Christ from the dead was manifested inside of them, and they were raised up into newness of life to become new creatures in Christ. *"For whom He did foreknow them He also did predestinate to be conformed"* (Romans 8:29). This word *"conform"* is the Greek word "*summorphos.*" It means "*to come out of the same mold, to be made according to a pattern.*" Jesus was the pattern, and when you were born again and made alive together with Christ, you came out of the same mold.

To illustrate consider this: if you make a recording on a CD, that CD is the master copy. If you put that CD into a duplicator with blank CDs loaded, you make perfect duplicates of the master. In Genesis 1:26 we read, "*Let us make man in our image.*" The word "*image*" means an "*exact duplication in kind.*" What does it mean to be in His image? We have been predestined to be formed in the image of Christ. Who was Christ? Christ was the very image of God. According to Hebrews 1:3, "*He is the express image of the invisible God.*" Jesus said, "*If you have seen Me you have seen the Father.*" He was man in the image of God, man as God intended man to be.

When you were born again, resurrected, and made alive together with Jesus, you became again what God intended Adam to be—man in the image of God. "*As Christ is, even so are we in this world*"(1 John 4:17). It is vital for you to have a revelation that you are "as Christ."

When Paul said you will be conformed to the image of Christ, he meant that you will emerge from the same mold as Christ. That happened when you were called, justified, and glorified in your spirit man. Your spirit man was made alive.

## Glorified

When Jesus rose from the dead He was glorified. John 7:39 reads, "*The Holy Spirit is not yet come because I have not yet been glorified,*" but when Jesus was glorified, He sent the Holy Ghost. When you were raised from the dead (when you were born again) you were glorified in your spirit with the same glory as Jesus. "*Christ in you the hope of glory*" (Colossians 1:27) .

Jesus walked in the glory, but the glory comes after a death and a resurrection. The Bible says in Hebrews 2:9-10 that "*Jesus suffered in order to be obedient to God.*" Hebrews 2:9 says, "*But we see Jesus who was made a little lower than the angels for the suffering of death crowned with glory and honor, crowned with glory, after the suffering of death, that He by the grace of*

*God might taste death for every man, for it was fitting for Him, for whom are all things and by whom are all things, and bringing many sons to glory."*

Glory is the manifest presence of God. We have been brought to glory, to the manifestation of the presence of God. *"Bringing many sons to glory, to make the captain of their salvation perfect through sufferings, for both he who sanctifies and those who are being sanctified are all of one family; one glory, for which reason He is not ashamed to call them brethren"* (Hebrews 2:10). We are all in God's family. Before we were born again we were in Adam's family, the living dead, but now we have passed from death to life so we are in the family of Almighty God. *"Behold what manner of love the Father has bestowed upon us that we should be called the sons of God"* (1 John 3:1).

> GLORY IS THE MANIFEST PRESENCE OF GOD.

This is New Testament Christianity, becoming sons of God, not just milk-toast church-goers, but sons of God. I am telling you who you are, what you have, what God has done, and your potential. I am telling you how to produce an abundant harvest in your life.

## Mature Saints

For too long the church has lived on milk. Some have received a little bit of bread, others a little bit more of the meat, but the Bible talks about the strong meat, (Hebrews 5:14) reserved for those who are mature. *"The whole creation is groaning and travailing, awaiting the manifestation of the sons of God"* (Romans 8:22-24). Creation is not waiting for Baptists, Methodists, Pentecostals, or Catholics, but for the sons of God. When the sons of God are manifest they will look like the Son found in Matthew, Mark, Luke, and John.

According to Romans 8:22-24, the whole creation is waiting for the church to grow up, for the church to find out who they are. Creation is waiting for the church to quit being religious, to cease going through the same rituals week after week producing no signs, wonders, miracles, salvations or deliverances. The antidote for this immature, weak church? To follow the Son of God. Then *"these signs shall follow"* (Mark 16:17).

When we are manifesting the sonship that is already ours, the glory follows us. When the glory follows us, people will follow us. Jesus drew a crowd everywhere He went because the glory was manifested in miracles, signs, and wonders. He said, *"You are conformed to My image. I am the firstborn of many."* You are one of the many. **We must take responsibility for who we are and for what God has done.**

The heartbeat of our ministry is to bring the church to maturity. The church (in her present state) is not getting the job done. This has to change. God has more to accomplish in this world. Our culture considers itself to be post-Christian. The church is pining for days when things were like they used to be. We want back the blessing, the peace, the joy that we could feel throughout the whole country. We had all that because there were great revivals, great movements birthed at the beginning of our nation. The heading of every preamble of every state constitution in this county is the same—all of them, bar none. "We owe it all to the almighty God, the benevolent Creator who has given us our rights." Every state constitution is written honoring and recognizing Almighty God. The reason we have a post-Christian culture is because the church ceased being the salt and the light of the earth. The church became religion. It got stuck in one time period and stopped being fresh in the Spirit, stopped moving ahead with God.

God is still speaking today, *"He that has an ear to hear, let him hear."* God is moving and things are happening. I have a burden to produce the kind of Christians the Bible talks about. I want to see people become like Matthew, Mark, Luke, and John. I want to be that way. Mature Christians are the ones who will accomplish God's purpose in this world.

## We are the Light of the World

He has brought many sons to glory, and we must accept responsibility for the work that God has already done. Many of us are straining to **become** what we already **are.** This is because we don't understand that God already did all of the work. *"We are the workmanship of God,* *created in Christ Jesus unto good works*" (Ephesians 2:10). We will never operate in those good works until we understand what kind of work God has already done in us.

**YOU WILL REPRODUCE WHATEVER YOU ARE.**

The seed produces after its own kind; the seed is in itself. You will reproduce whatever you are, you can't reproduce what you're not. We have been recreated in the image of God; spiritually it's already done. So what is our problem?

Proverbs 20:27 says, "*The Spirit of man is the candle of the Lord, searching all the inward parts of the belly.*" John 1:4 says, "*In Him was life, and the life was the light of men.*" That candle was dark before Jesus died to become the light of life. Jesus is the light of life. He brought eternal life into us. Our candle which sat in darkness, is now lit, so we have the light, and the brightness of His glory is shining on the inside of us.

Why isn't your light bright? You were born again, and filled with the Holy Ghost. The candle is lit, but for some reason you find yourself still conformed to the world. You are a Christian (culturally) but not a mature Bible Christian. If you take your values from the world, from the godless, instead of from the Bible and the godly, then your mind is not yet renewed. God did His work in you, but your perception of who you are and who God is in your life has not changed. You have been born again and filled with the Spirit, but have not really comprehended what has transpired.

*"You cannot light a candle and put it under a bushel basket"* (Matthew 5:15). The light will go out. God put a light in us. He lit our candle, but there is a bushel basket on our head. That means as long as your mind is uninformed about who you are in Christ and what God has done in you, the light that is on the inside of you is shrouded; it can't shine. The light is not revealed even though it is in you. Jesus said, *"I am the light of the world"* (John 8:12). He also said, *"You are the light of the world"* (Matthew 5:14).

That light does not come from New Age philosophies. That light comes from one person—Jesus Christ. *"He who has the Son has life, and he who has not the Son has not life"* (John 3:36). You might have religion, you might have beliefs, but if you do not have Jesus Christ, you do not have life.

## Our Life is a Seed that Must be Planted

We are now seed which must be planted. Jesus was the seed, now He has made many brethren. We are just like Him. Now we must follow Him. He said, *"Where the master is, there the servant will be also."* (John 12:26). We must follow Him to the cross and into the grave. We follow Him to the planting of our life in order to reap an abundant harvest. We are now the seed that must be planted, *"Unless a kernel of wheat falls into the ground and dies, it remains alone."* It bears no fruit, produces no harvest, has no productivity, no multiplication, just one lonely dormant seed with no joy or victory. Joy comes from looking for a harvest. Joy does not come by consumerism or from getting everything you want from God. Joy comes from the promise of the harvest.

Paul said, *"For the joy that was set before Him."* There is no joy in being a materialistic person, or a consumer

Christian. We were created to reproduce, to multiply.

Until you see the harvest there is no joy. Because your life was planted, you have an expectation of the harvest coming in your life. You have joy!

**BECAUSE YOUR LIFE WAS PLANTED, YOU HAVE AN EXPECTATION OF THE HARVEST. YOU HAVE JOY!**

There are Christians who are born again, who are even filled with the Spirit, but who remain dormant. They are unplanted seeds. John 12:25 describes the process of death: *"He who loves his life will lose it; he who hates his life in this world will keep it for eternal life. If anyone serves Me let him follow Me and where I am there My servant will be also. Anyone who serves Me will My Father honor."* I want God's honor. That honor is harvest multiplication. It is the productive life.

## The Seed Must Die

Jesus began describing the process of death by saying, *"Unless a kernel of wheat falls in the ground and dies it remains alone, but if it dies, it's going to bring forth much fruit*." Next He explained how this happens. All four of the Gospel writers were led to explain this principle. When God talks a lot about something it's important, and we should pay attention to it. This principle of seedtime and harvest is repeated over and over again in the Gospels.

**YOU WILL NOT HAVE ABUNDANT FRUIT IN YOUR LIFE UNLESS YOU DIE.**

This is an absolute. You cannot be a productive Christian unless you die. You can be born again and filled with the Spirit, but you won't have abundant fruit in your life unless you die.

Some people are willing to die and some are not. Some people are afraid to die. They hold on to their life, preserving and protecting it, but they are miserable. Jesus said, *"He who tries to save his life will lose it."* You will not have joy when you hold on, afraid to die, afraid to trust Jesus with your whole being. I have seen people give up because they wouldn't die. They give up on the church, give up on God, and say, "Well, I tried it but it just didn't do anything for me." They would not die to themselves and become alive in Christ. This is the heart of the message of the Gospel: the death, burial and resurrection of Jesus.

Every seed has a tiny plant inside. But seeds are dormant until they are planted. The seed coat is the hard shell on the outside of the seed. Some seed coats are thicker and harder than others. Some are thinner and not quite as hard. Before planting seeds with a hard shell they need to be soaked in water to first soften the shell. This helps the seed die easily in the soil so it can sprout.

When you were born again, God filled you with the Holy Ghost so He could soak you for a while before planting you. He filled you with the Spirit to get you wet so you could die. You don't need to get touched again, to receive a new anointing, or to get in this river and in that river. You don't need to keep getting wet. You don't need to come to church every week just to get your blessing.

While planting churches in the Carolinas, I remember how some folks came to church and said, "Well, I came for my blessing today." Then when they were leaving they would say, "I got my blessing." I wanted to say, "But did you die yet? You have been coming for ten years saying the same thing, 'I got my blessing, I got wet again, I jumped in the water, I got wet again.' I want to know when you are going to get in the garden to plant yourself, to sow your life into the gospel of Jesus Christ."

Many Christians have "blessing issues." They run around everywhere trying to get another blessing. They have been in church for awhile, but they are empty. They got blessed and blessed, but they still have no joy, no peace. They blame this on the church, but the problem is theirs—they refuse to die. Instead they say, "I need to go over here to this church and get another blessing. I heard the Spirit is really moving over there." You have to get rid of that hard seed coat, you have to die to self.

You have to die. Jesus did. You are filled with the Spirit as preparation for planting by shedding that hard-shell life, the self-centered loving of self. Jesus said, "He that loves his life shall lose it." The seed coat causes you to say, "I love my life so much that I'm going to hold onto it, protect it, and not plant it. I refuse to die." After awhile you get sick and tired of the miserable life you live—alone, outside of God's way.

"Unless it falls in the ground and dies, it remains alone." Some think Christianity is boring. It's not. It is exciting to have followers of your own—people you brought to salvation and disciples you are mentoring. It's exciting when God flows through you so a miracle happens—a blind eye is opened, or a deaf ear is opened, a marriage is saved, families are turned around, and kids are delivered. Life becomes exciting and you have joy unspeakable, full of glory!

## More Than Enough

For many who are just starting out, the pay may not great in ministry—but seedtime and harvest is great. I don't live by my paycheck because it wouldn't be enough. I live by my giving and I have more than enough. Some think because I have two cars, a motorcycle, a motor home, and five houses that I must be stealing the church's money. I get a pay check like everyone else, but extra money just comes to me. Blessings come upon you and overtake you. It's called the honor of God.

He said, "*Whoever loves his life shall lose it, but whoever loses his life for My sake and the gospel shall find it*" (Matthew 10:39). There are two Greek words for life in these passages of scripture. There is the "*psyche*" life which refers to your "*self life*," and then there is "*zoe*" which is the divine life. Jesus was saying, "If you lose your *psyche* you're going to get the *zoe*—the eternal life of God." Zoe, the divine eternal life of God, will be manifested in you if you are willing to lose your self life. That is the dying.

How do we let this old shell be broken so that new life can emerge, spring up, grow, and multiply? How can your life multiply the seed in itself? As I become a full-grown plant there is more seed produced in my life. Mark 8:34 demonstrates a practical application to dying and planting your life. It says, "*When He had called the people to Himself with His disciples also He said to them, 'Whoever desires to come after Me let him deny himself, take up his cross and follow Me. For whoever desires to save his life will lose it, but he that loses his life for My sake and the gospel's, shall find it. For what will it profit a man if he gains the whole world and loses* his own soul?  Or what will a man gain in exchange for his soul?'"

## Die to Your Reputation

Jesus said that I have to be willing to identify with Him, for His sake, and for the Gospel.  In Mark 8:38 He talks about being ashamed of Him.  He said, *"If you're ashamed of Me, then I'm going to be ashamed of you."*  By saying this, Jesus revealed that the first thing in us that must die is our reputation. This means I must identify with Jesus Christ openly.  I must speak His Word publicly, letting people know I'm a Christian; that Jesus is my Savior and my Lord.  Others should know that I live by the principles of the Holy Word of God. You have to die to what you want others to think of you.

If I acknowledge I am a Christian, then I am going to be persecuted.  I have to die to what I want others to think of me.  I say some things that I know it might make some people a little upset. I had to get delivered before I could help people. I had to get delivered from my love of self, from loving myself more than loving others. When I love you I cannot hold back what I need to tell you because I'm afraid you will think evil of me. I'm going to say what I need to so you can be whole, and let you think whatever you are going to think. I must care for you more than I care about what you think of me. It's called dying. If you are not willing to do that, you are a dormant seed.

Matthew 10:34 says, "Do not think that I am come to bring peace on earth. I did not come to bring peace but a sword; for I have come to set a man against his father, a daughter against her mother, and daughter-in-law against her mother-in-law. A man's enemies will be those in his own household. He who loves father and mother more than Me is not worthy of Me, and he who loves son or daughter more than Me is not worthy of Me." Jesus continues, "and he that does not take up his cross and follow Me is not worthy of Me." He is saying that you must die to your reputation.

**YOU MUST DIE TO YOUR REPUTATION.**

# Die to Your Relationships

Your relationships are the next thing that must die. **The most intimate relationships you have cannot come between you and Jesus Christ.** If you identify with Christ, if you take up your cross, really die and plant yourself, then sometimes your husband, or wife, or children shun or persecute you. It will create some division in your home, but Jesus said, "If you are not willing to die and sacrifice relationship and put it in His hands, you are not worthy of Me." I've had to do it with my own sons and daughters. When the boys were living at home and started manifesting rebellion against God, I said, "Boys, you will have to move out of the house if you continue to be a bad example to your sisters. I have to protect the girls. Make your choice." Was that hard? Absolutely. Very hard, and I did it. Now they are both on my staff in ministry, preaching the Gospel. They know I was right. They learned from it. Everybody learned from it, and it brought the fear of God in our house.

I had to decide to be loyal to Jesus first. Husbands do not come before Jesus. Wives do not come before

Jesus. Children do not come before Jesus, and Grandma does not come before Jesus. No one comes before Jesus. We have to be loyal to Jesus first. He said, "If you won't put Me first and be loyal to Me above every other intimate relationship you may have, you are not worthy of Me." Jesus can say this because when He died, He was our example of giving up relationship. He gave up His intimate relationship with the Father for you, and hung on a cross and said, *"My God, My God why has thou forsaken Me?"* He was willing to sacrifice the most intimate relationship He had for you. He can say, "Look, I did it, and if you are not willing to do what I did, you are not worthy of Me."

**NO ONE COMES BEFORE JESUS.**

## Die to Your Rights

There are three things to which you must die: your reputation, your relationships, and your rights. You have to put Jesus first and be loyal to Him above everything.

"But it's my life. What if God wants me to do something I don't want to do?"

Die.

"What if God wants me to go where I don't want to go?"

Die.

You have to give up the right to your own life. Why? It is not yours, it belongs to God by right of creation and by right of redemption. You are no longer your own, you no longer have a choice.

At the Last Supper, Jesus was speaking about eating His flesh and drinking His blood. He said *"I tell you the truth, unless you eat the flesh of the Son of Man and drink his blood; you have no life in you"* (John 6:53). These were hard sayings and the Bible reports that from this time many of His disciples no longer followed Him. When you begin to get into some of these things, people think about the hard sayings of Jesus. God already did His part. The hard part for you is dying—taking up your cross, dying, and planting your life. How can you do this?

For the joy that is set before you—God's honor coming upon your life. God giving you an abundant harvest.

## An Abundant Harvest Now

I am resurrected in glory now, not just when I die. I get to walk in the glory and presence of Almighty God. I am referring to walking in it, not just receiving a blessing. I am talking about walking in the glory every day of your life. Jesus walked in the glory. In John 2, when Jesus turned the water to wine, *"He manifested forth His glory."* Miracles are a result of walking in the glory of God. It is not my life. Jesus said, *"Not My will but Thine be done."* I'm bought with a price, so I surrender all my rights to God. I no longer have a choice, I defer all my choices to God; I died.

**MIRACLES ARE A RESULT OF WALKING IN THE GLORY OF GOD.**

When I was in South Carolina, I had a beautiful home on Lady's Island right down the road from the beach. That was where I wanted to be and God sent me there.

We planted a church there and then God called me to go back to West Virginia. I set all my plans aside. I do not know when I will get to do what I want to do; sail my sailboat and ride the coastal waterways on my motorcycle. I had to put everything I want to do way off somewhere. I returned to Fairmont. I died. I planted myself and I'm having the time of my life being blessed by Almighty God. God is honoring me. It is His honor.

You must take up your cross. That means planting your life in Christ with loyalty to Jesus first—above yourself and others. This is what makes life really full, abundant, and productive. This will result in God's honor. The glory is released in you and an abundant harvest will follow.

# How to Plant Your Life as a Seed

# STUDY GUIDE

## Chapter Four Summary

*In chapters one through three we have learned:*

- *Both the natural and the spiritual realms revolve around the principle of seedtime and harvest.*

- *How to plant the Word of God into our heart.*

- *How to plant the seed of faith with our words.*

- *How to plant financial seed for a money harvest.*

*In chapter four we learned that **we must plant our life as a seed** just as Jesus did. **Like Jesus, we must die so that we may reproduce.** We must die to self. We must put Jesus first in our life—above our family, above ourselves, above our friends, and above the pleasures of the world.*

Because of Adam's sin, man was lost. God sent His Son, Jesus, to shed His blood and redeem us (buy us back). Jesus' life became seed. When we accept Jesus as our Savior, we are the fruit of that seed. We become part of the family of God. We then plant our seed (our life) to bring forth more sons of God. **We must accept the responsibility of being what God has called us to be, so that we may plant seeds and bring forth Christians who will accomplish God's purpose in this world.**

*Fill in the blanks. There is an answer key provided on page 139 at the end of this book.*

1. Jesus told his disciples in Mark 8:34 that "whosever will come after me, let him _____ himself, and take up his _____, and follow me."

2. We must let others know that Jesus is our Savior and if we are ashamed of Him, He will be _____ of us.

3. We must sow our life into the Gospel of _____.

4. Jesus said, "If you have seen me you have seen the

   _____ ." He was _____

   in the image of God. When we become born again,

   we have been recreated in the _____

   of God.

5. In order to produce, seeds must _____ ;

   "Unless it falls in the ground and dies, it remains

   _____ ." As Christians, we must die

   to flesh daily so that we can produce a _____ .

   We are to go forth as the disciples of Jesus and

   produce _____ who will become

   _____ .

6. By right of _____ , our life belongs

   to God. We are no longer our own, we no longer

   have a choice. By planting our _____ as

   a seed, God will give us an abundant _____ .

# STUDY GUIDE ANSWER KEY

## Chapter One Answers: Planting the Seed of the Word in your Heart

1. Christ
   fruitful and productive
   seedtime and harvest

2. counsel
   sinners
   seat of the scornful
   mediate
   tree
   rivers
   prosper

3. incorruptible
   Word
   seed
   Jesus

4. information

   revelation

   impartation

## Chapter Two Answers: Planting the Seed of Faith With Words

1. seedtime

   harvest

2. phenomenon
   principle
   phenomenon
   principle

3. words

4. Word
   faith
   confession
   faith
   wavering

5. covenant

   covenant

# Chapter Three Answers: Planting the Seed of Money for Financial Harvest

1. servant
   servants
   steward
   prosperity
   lazy
   work
   eat

2. tithing
   ten percent
   church you attend
   meat

3. offering
   reap
   sow

4. windows
   blessing
   devourer
   blessed

# Chapter Four Answers: How to Plant Your Life as a Seed

1. deny

   cross

2. ashamed

3. Jesus Christ

4. Father

   man

   image

5. die

   alone

   harvest

   followers

   disciples

# REVIVAL FELLOWSHIP INTERNATIONAL

## CALLING & PURPOSE DEFINED

God has promised the *"restoration of all things"*...

*"Repent ye therefore, and be converted, that your sins may be blotted out, when the times of refreshing shall come from the presence of the Lord; and He shall send Jesus Christ, which before was preached unto you: Whom the heaven must receive until the times of restoration of all things, which God has spoken by the mouth of all His holy prophets since the world began."*

—Acts 3:19-21

We understand this scripture means that all scriptural truth (Colossians 1:9) and gifts and ministries of the Holy Spirit (Ephesians 4:11; 1 Corinthians 12:28) will be known and working in the church before Jesus returns bodily to earth. This restoration will result in worldwide revival bringing in the harvest of the former and latter rains (James 5:7), and prepare for the coming of Jesus to reign as King of Kings throughout the millennial government being established now in the church upon the earth (Isaiah 9:6-7).

Revival Fellowship International (RFI) was birthed by God in 1995 as a result of the calling and preparation of Dr. John Polis, beginning with a vision given during a season of fasting and prayer in January 1983. During this time of fasting and prayer, John was shown a *"sheet of rain"* falling with large drops interspersed in the downpour. The Holy Spirit said, *"the large drops are five fold ministry gifts and this will be a latter rain movement."* With this vision in mind, John set out to see it fulfilled from 1983-1994 while serving in a main-line Pentecostal denomination. During this time, God was preparing him for an apostolic leadership role in the Body of Christ. After a long season (14 years) in the desert of preparation, and with the help of devoted friends called to help, God released John to form the *"new wineskin"* called Revival Fellowship International which continues to grow nationally and internationally through divine connections and appointments.

Among the apostolic responsibilities given to RFI is one of ensuring that believers are schooled in all truth being restored to the church (1 Thessalonians 3:9-10). As we look at church history from 1500 until now, we see a progressive revelation of Biblical truth falling into four categories: Evangelical, Pentecostal, Charismatic, and Kingdom Theology.

## The Evangelical Movement

The Evangelical Movement embraces *"milk of the word"* doctrines (I Peter 2:1-2), those which are the first needed and easiest to understand such as: the New Birth, Water Baptism, the Return of Jesus, Final Judgment, and the Infallibility of Scripture. It consists of main-line Protestant denominations.

## The Pentecostal Movement

The Pentecostal Movement went a *"little deeper"* in revelation by receiving the truth of the Baptism in the Holy

Spirit with all nine gifts in manifestation, and a doctrine of Sanctification, or *"holy living."* This led to the Healing Revivals of the mid 1900's.

## The Charismatic Movement

Then came the Charismatic Movement which brought the *"meat of The Word"* teaching ( 1 Corinthians 3:2). This includes such things as: the Word of Faith message, Positional Truths, Davidic Worship, and Prosperity.

## Kingdom Theology

The *"present truth"* (2 Peter 1:12) message called Kingdom Theology teaches Divine Government, Five Fold Ministries, Spiritual Warfare, Intercession, and Spiritual Fathering. All of these are are *"strong meat"* messages (Hebrews 5:11-14).

## Restoration Theology

What we call Restoration Theology encompasses the truth revealed in *each* movement, bringing all the streams together into a mighty river of God.

> *"There is a river, the streams whereof make glad the city of God (church)."*                    Psalm 46:4

This is what the Apostle Paul meant when he told the Thessalonians "I long to see you again and supply what is lacking in your faith" (I Thessalonians 3:10). Simply put, this means to complete their understanding of God's Word.

RFI is called to preach and teach (Colossians 1:25-28) **Restoration Theology** to the Body of Christ, presenting *"every man complete in Christ."* This is being done through camp meeting, conferences, publications, media, newsletters, and Bible Colleges at home and abroad.

A second apostolic responsibility of RFI is in the raising up of a new generation of leaders as *"spiritual sons and daughters"* who will lead Restoration Revival as it continues until Jesus returns to earth. RFI offers a credentialing process that brings people into covenant relationships necessary for impartation to take place.

The Elijah anointing has been imparted to RFI and is the generational inheritance given to those in covenant connection with the movement. This end time anointing imparts Prophetic Intercession, Passion for God, Power Gifts, Paternal Anointing, and Prosperity. All of these characteristics are identifiable in the life of Elijah (I Kings 17-19). Those apostolic leaders with an Elijah anointing are the true spiritual fathers in today's church.

By running with this vision, RFI is fulfilling the prophecy of restoration found in Acts 3:19-21:

> *"...Heaven must retain Him until the times*
> *of restoration of all things."*

As a spiritual house being built by God (Psalm 127:1; I Chronicles 17:10-14), RFI provides safe spiritual covering, covenant relationship, networking, supportive ministry, and corporate vision of world proportions. You are invited to partner with RFI in the call & vision God has given.

REVIVAL FELLOWSHIP
INTERNATIONAL
P.O. Box 1007 | Beaufort, SC 29901
w w w . r f i u s a . o r g

# THE KINGS ARE COMING
## B O O K

Find out about the 4 characteristics of the coming Kings. Kingly anointing is being released now!

- The Wisdom of Kings
- The Character of Kings
- The Power of Kings
- The Wealth of Kings

**64 Pages:**................... **Price: $8**

# RECYCLED BELIEVERS
## B O O K

Find the answers to the following questions:

- Why does God move Christians to a different church?
- How do today's transient Christians relate to people in the Bible?
- Does God really call Christians to "get connected"?
- What are the four categories of "migrating sheep" in today's church?
- How do you find your "place of release" in another's ministry?
- How do you enjoy continual revival?

**64 Pages:**................... **Price: $8**

# APOSTOLIC ADVICE
## B O O K

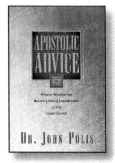

Proven wisdom for building strong foundations in the local church.

**107 Pages:** ................... **Price: $8**

# RELEASE THE RIVER WITHIN YOU
## B O O K

The Church of Jesus Christ is moving into "deep waters" of the Spirit. According to Ezekiel's vision of the "River of God," there are ever-increasing levels of anointing starting with the "ankles" all the way to "waters to swim in." Learn about the progression from the Prophetic, to the Priestly, and then to the Kingly Anointing.

**118 Pages:** . . . . . . . . . . . . . . . . . . . . . **Price: $8**

# TAKE MY YOKE UPON YOU
## B O O K

We each have a "three-dimensional" destiny—a destiny in the Body of Christ, a destiny in the local church, and an individual destiny. Fulfillment of your three-dimensional destiny depends upon your willingness to employ your God-given talents and gifts by responding to the invitation of Jesus to *TAKE MY YOKE UPON YOU.*

**95 Pages:** . . . . . . . . . . . . . . . . . . . . . . **Price: $8**

# BOOK BUNDLE
## P A C K A G E

5 Great Titles from Dr. John Polis

> Release The River Within You
> Apostolic Advice
> Take My Yoke Upon You
> The Kings Are Coming
> Recycled Believers

**5 Books:** . . . . . . . . . . . . . . . . . . . . . . **Price: $30**

# THE COMPLETE SCHOOL OF FATIH
## P A C K A G E

This series of messages was originally intended to be a one hour teaching for a Wednesday night Bible study. God poured out His Spirit for 13 weeks with divine revelation and a fresh look at faith which has inspired hundreds thus far.

**13 CD Series:** . . . . . . . . . . . . . . . **Price: $40**
**13 DVD Series:** . . . . . . . . . . . . . . . **Price: $50**

# FAITH
## P A C K A G E

Faith is the most important subject. This series offers revelation and an impartation of the spirit of faith.

- The Sixth Sense (2 CDs)
- Thy Faith (1 CD)
- Obtaining The Gift Of Faith (1 CD)
- Let Us Hold Fast (1 CD)
- Take The Limits Off (1 CD)

**6 CD Package:** . . . . . . . . . . . . . . . **Price: $20**

# CLASSIC REVIVAL
## P A C K A G E

- Getting Ready For The Final Harvest (1 CD)
- Can Anyone Eat From Your Dish? (1 CD)
- Life Can Be Dangerous (1 CD)
- Perilous Times Shall Come (1 CD)
- End Time Revival (1 CD)

**5 CD Package:** . . . . . . . . . . . . . . . . . **Price: $20**

# HEALING
## P A C K A G E

- Seven Reasons Why Healing Is For Today (1 CD)
- Where Does Sickness Come From? (1 CD)
- Redeemed From The Curse (1 CD)
- God Will Heal You (Six half-hour sessions on 2 DVDs plus Syllabus on CD-ROM)

**Package Contains:**
**3 CDs, 2 DVDs, 1 CD-ROM: . . . . . . Price: $20**

# PROSPERITY
## P A C K A G E

- God's Reward Program (1 CD)
- How To Produce Abundance In Your Life (1 CD)
- The Kings Are Coming (1 CD)
- Obtaining Overflow (1 CD)

**4 CD Package: . . . . . . . . . . . . . . Price: $20**

# SPIRITUAL FATHERING
## P A C K A G E

- Sifted Sons (1 cd)
- Climbing The King's Mountain (1 cd)
- The Elijah Anointing (1 cd)
- Freedom From The Orphan Spirit (1 cd)
- Keys To Maturity (1 cd)

**5 CD Package: . . . . . . . . . . . . . . . . Price: $20**

# DIVINE ORDER
## P A C K A G E

God is restoring order and government to the church.

- Catching Up With God (3 CDs)
  Four Main Truths of the Present Restoration
- Biblical Headship (5 CDs)
  Study of the Origin and Operation of Eldership
- God's Government (3 CDs)
  Apostles, Elders, Deacons, and Saints

**11 CD Series:** . . . . . . . . . . . . . . . . . .**Price: $20**

# APOSTOLIC RESTORATION
## P A C K A G E

Dr. John explains the functions and anointing of the apostle based on Scripture and twenty-five years of apostolic experience.

- The Ministry of the Apostle (5 cds)
- Apostolic Transition (1 cd)
- Apostolic Prioities (1 cd)

**7 CD Series:** . . . . . . . . . . . . . . . . . **Price: $20**

To check current prices on all resources by
Dr. John Polis, or to place an order:

# 1.843.322.0363

John Polis Ministries
PO Box 1007
Beaufort SC 29901

Email: drjohn@rfiusa.org

## www.rfiusa.org